Sweet Joymaker

SWEET JOYMAKER

A SECOND CHANCE SEASONED ROMANCE

JEAN ORAM

ORAM PRODUCTIONS

Sweet Joymaker

A Second Chance Seasoned Romance
Indigo Bay Christmas Romances (Book 3)
By Jean Oram

© 2020 Jean Oram
First Edition

Cover Designed by Najla Qamber Designs

All characters and events appearing in this book are fictitious. Any resemblance to real people, alive or dead, as well as any resemblance to events is coincidental unless your name is Travis, in which case… you're welcome. And if your name rhymes with Donna… enjoy the laughs and sorry about the triplets. Thank goodness they're fictional.

Printed in the United States of America unless otherwise stated on the last page of this book. Published by Oram Productions Alberta, Canada.

Complete LIBRARY OF CONGRESS CATALOGING-IN-PUBLICATION DATA available online or by request.

Oram, Jean.

Sweet Joymaker / Jean Oram.—1st. ed.

ISBN 978-1-989359-20-4, 978-1-989359-21-1 (paperback)

Ebook ISBN (primary) 978-1-989359-19-8

First Oram Productions Edition: October 2020

1020

Maria's story is one I started months and months before it was "her turn" in my production schedule. I poked at her story here and there, adding words and fussing and fretting that maybe she didn't actually have a story after all.

It wasn't until I was writing her son Ryan's story, The Cowboy's Second Chance, that Maria's story began to truly take form. Their conversations began to crossover between the two books, and you may even recognize a scene in this book that you can also find in The Cowboy's Second Chance (The Cowboys of Sweetheart Creek, Texas Book 3).

But like in life, every conversation has two sides, and so do Maria and Ryan's scenes. They both get different things from that one conversation. And while it is shown in both books, they are two very different scenes, and both characters take different lessons from each other.

One conversation, two scenes, two completely different takes and outcomes. But don't worry, they both find the courage to reclaim the love they're in the process of losing due to their fears.

Because that's what it's all really about, isn't it? Finding love. Overcoming our fears. Living our best life with hearts full of joy.

That's what Maria's story is about, and I hope as you read it, it fills your heart with hope and warmth.

Happy reading.

Jean Oram
Canada, October 2020

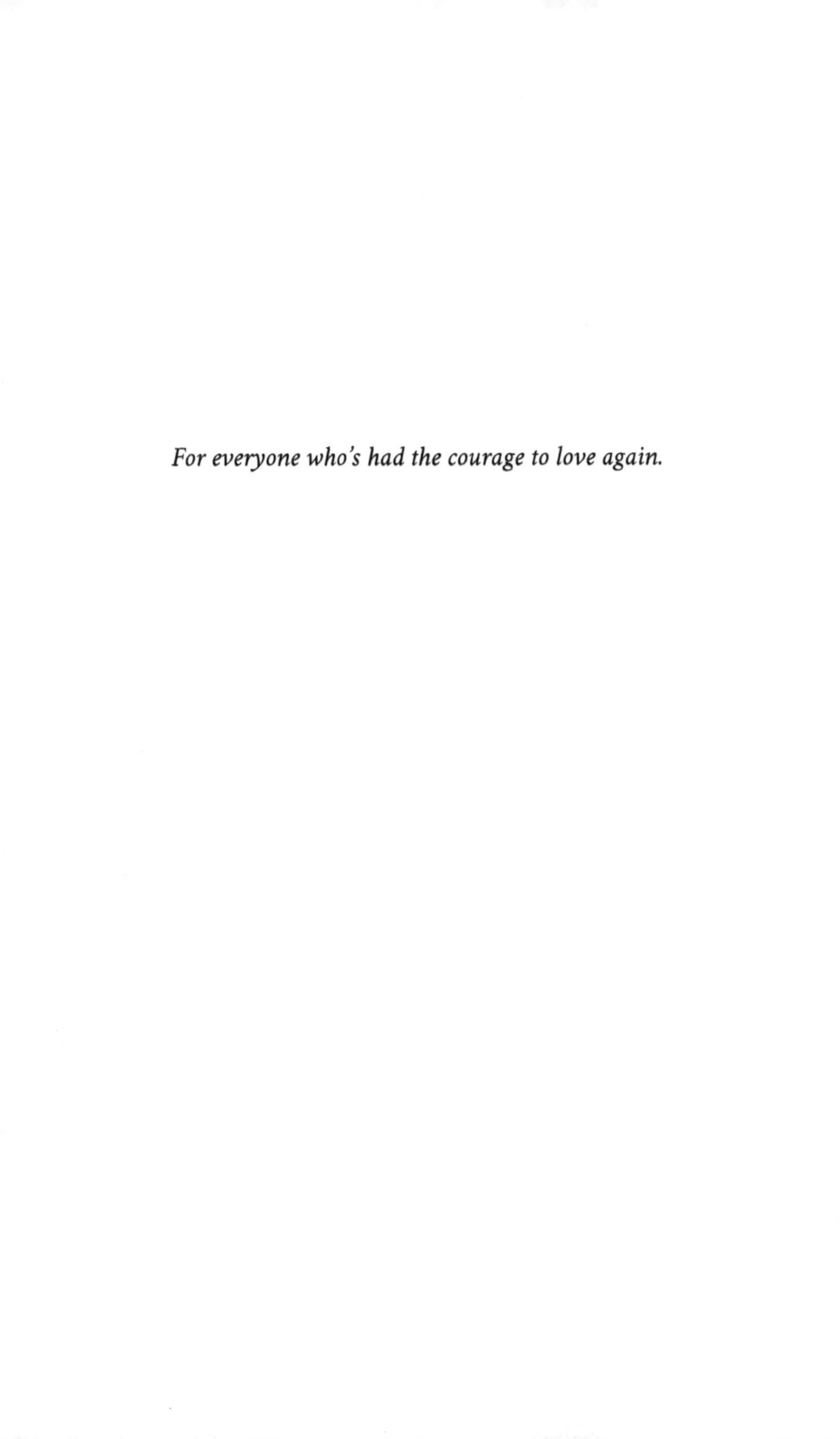

For everyone who's had the courage to love again.

ACKNOWLEDGMENTS

Thank you to the authors of Indigo Bay, past and present, and in particular to Kay Correll for allowing me to join, then coordinate this world. I've discovered so many new characters, made many new author friends along the way, as well as found so many delightful new readers that I cherish dearly.

A special thank you also goes to the team who help me attack the swings and misses from my dear editor Margaret C. to my error finding team. You're the best!

$\mathcal{M}$aria Wylder sat in the Longhorn Diner in Sweetheart Creek, Texas, and let the hubbub swirl around her. Everyone wanted to chat about her sons Myles and Ryan, and their high school football team. Since they'd begun coaching a few years ago, they'd taken several runs at the state championship, and this year was no different. It was exciting, but the way the playoffs extended their season so close to Christmas left everyone exhausted. Or was that only her?

Christmas carols played on the local radio station, creating a seasonal backdrop to the diner's usual sounds of clattering dishes and neighbors chatting about their cattle.

Maria's friend Fiona Fisher hoisted a full pot of coffee from her spot behind the back counter. "Top up, hon?" She poked at her teased, bleached hair with her free hand.

"I'm good for now, thanks."

"Muffin?"

Maria shook her head and Fiona watched her for a second before moving along. The waitress was good at picking up on her moods, the two of them having served as each other's rock since elementary school. Maria didn't want to count the years. She winced as her mind completed the mental math despite her wishes at avoidance. Close to a half century.

Half a *century*.

Could she feel any older?

"Did you hear he got a clean bill of health?" Fiona asked a few moments later as she hurried past with the empty coffeepot and a dirty plate. There was no doubt in Maria's mind why her friend stayed so slim. She probably logged twenty thousand steps as she served tables each day.

"Who got a clean bill of health?"

"Clint."

At the mechanic's name, Maria's heart picked up its pace. Clint Walker was a sweetheart. One of the few good ones. He'd gone out of his way since her somewhat recent divorce to make her feel special, beautiful and wanted. If they were younger, she'd consider dating again.

But they were well past the age where idealistic hopes and dreams for the future had a place in their lives. There were ranches and businesses to tend to, and families to care for. After Roy, her husband of thirty-seven years, had asked for a divorce a year ago, Maria had moved off the family ranch and focused on herself, like everyone said she was supposed to.

She'd been bored, and after Roy had moved into town as well, their sons had struggled with running the family ranch while keeping up with things such as meals. Her boys had needed her there, supporting, helping, guiding. And since she'd moved back a few months ago, they'd been doing better and she'd been happier, full of purpose. She didn't have time to date.

"I didn't realize he was having health issues," she said to Fiona.

"Just a scare. We're getting to that age."

Seriously? How had she become this old without noticing? Maybe if she had grandkids it would feel okay to be staring down fifty-nine, knowing the big six-O was waiting right behind it.

"Well, I'm glad he's okay." Maria ran her fingers over one of her long feather earrings and shivered. She didn't spend much time with Clint, but would have missed him had his health scare been more than that.

"Good afternoon, ladies," said a rich, deep voice as a man took a seat two down from Maria. Garfield Goodwin smiled at her, his dentures big and white. The smile warmed, reaching his eyes, when Fiona turned to look at him.

"Hello, Garfield," she said, fussing with her hair again as color brightened her cheeks. "The usual?"

"Yes, my dear."

She thrust out a hip. "What have I said about using terms of endearment?"

"Come on, Fiona," he said, his tone low and coaxing. "They make you feel young."

The waitress rolled her eyes and set about preparing his muffin and coffee.

Every day Garfield came in, flirted with Fiona and left a tip so big she always protested. Garfield was single. Fiona was married—not quite happily—but Maria worried Garfield wasn't entirely harmless. She often found herself wishing he would take a hint and leave her friend alone.

A man with flyaway hair sat down on Maria's other side, and she groaned internally. It was her ex-husband's uncle, the town grump, Henry Wylder. Why couldn't she have lost him in the divorce?

"I'm having a Christmas party, and y'all are welcome," Henry announced, his words coming out more like a challenge than an invitation anyone might jump to accept.

"That's nice," Maria said, reminding herself to be pleasant. Always be pleasant. In a small town you never knew when you might need to rely on your enemy, so it was best not to have any.

"Good for you, getting into the spirit of things," Garfield said. "Only took you about ninety years."

"I'm only sixty-nine," Henry grumbled. "You're welcome to attend," he said to Maria, his tone still gruff.

She shifted uncomfortably on her stool. "Thank you."

She'd heard he was planning a party, and had hoped to avoid receiving an invitation, since she was fairly certain Roy would be there. Along with his new wife, Sophia.

"It's this Saturday."

"Day after the semifinals game. Go Torpedoes!" Garfield said, and nearby diners let out a whoop for her boys' football team.

"I invited Roy, too." Henry continued as though he hadn't been interrupted.

"That's nice," she said mildly. She caught Fiona's eye and pushed her empty coffee cup away so she could collect it. "Can I get a peppermint tea, please?"

Her friend frowned, but went to fetch her hot water.

"So?" Henry asked. "Are you coming?"

"I'm not sure."

"What aren't you sure about?"

Maria had nothing against Sophia, but she wasn't prepared to go to Henry's party and pretend to be happy about it. Especially with her ex-husband and his new wife kissing in the corner. It just felt… wrong. Too soon. She'd spent far too many years being the one Roy kissed at parties, and to see him kiss someone else still took her breath away, the feeling of betrayal too far ingrained to shrug off even though he was within his rights.

It was probably time for her to get used to the idea, since

the divorce had been finalized last February and Roy had remarried in June. He'd stayed on the ranch until the wedding, then moved into Sweetheart Creek, population 4,123.

As far as she was concerned, that was too small for the two of them. It felt as though Roy and Sophia had taken over every corner of town. Back when Maria was still living in an apartment a few blocks from their new home and not having sunrise chores, it had all been too much. Luckily, the boys had welcomed her back on the ranch even though it had sent Roy into a tizzy he still hadn't quite gotten over.

"Well?" Henry demanded, waiting for her decision.

If she went to his party, she'd be alone. Awkwardly alone.

But she didn't want someone new. It took too much energy to face men coming and going, and ultimately leaving. And Henry's Christmas party invitation wasn't the only one coming up in the following week. There were several. And Roy would be at all of them, since his retired butt had nothing better to do.

"I was thinking I might visit a friend," Maria said, hoping the fib wasn't too obvious.

"I invited the boys," Henry said, referring to her sons. "But Levi said he's going to be out of town with that model of his."

Darn her firstborn and his quick thinking. She'd bet he hadn't had plans before the invitation.

"Her name is Laura," Maria said, referring to Levi's girlfriend. Her boys were getting to the age where, as her father-in-law had said, they were pairing up like there was an ark parked on Main Street and the rain had started. Levi and Myles were both in new, committed relationships, and she had a feeling that Ryan, her youngest, was getting pretty cozy with the ranch's new neighbor, Carly Clarke.

She hoped her boys stayed the course and didn't break any hearts, like men on both sides of the family had a tendency to do. Both Roy and her father had been heart-breakers, and she hoped that wherever her second-born son, Cole, was at the moment, he was being good to women's hearts.

Maria shook her head, trying to find a happier mood. This would be the first Christmas where she'd be sharing her boys not only with their girlfriends and their families, but with Sophia, too.

How was any of that supposed to work?

"So? Are you coming?" Henry demanded. "I need to know how many people to expect and I don't have time for wishy-washy replies. The party's in three days."

"No, I'm not, thank you," Maria said, her tone more brusque than she'd intended.

Henry stilled, then turned to face her. "After all I've done for your library, and you can't even come to my Christmas party?"

Maria inhaled slowly, struggling for calm. Henry hadn't done much for the town library last month. It had been her son Myles and his girlfriend, Karen, who had done the heavy lifting to save the building. Meanwhile, Henry had practically thrown a barricade in front of their plans.

"I'm sorry. I'll be away," she told him, as a plan formed in her mind. An old friend, Kittim Lane, had been trying to convince her to visit her in Indigo Bay, South Carolina. She was busy helping with an upcoming fundraiser for the coastal town's animal shelter, and had suggested Maria come let her hair down at the gala. She'd said no, due to the timing of the gala, as her boys' team would be playing in the Texas football state championship game the day prior, but maybe Kittim needed some help leading up to the fundraiser.

Either way, getting away might be exactly what she needed right now. And not just because she'd avoid facing

Roy at a million Christmas parties they used to attend together.

"Where are you going?" Henry demanded.

"Indigo Bay." The prospect of spending time near the ocean while visiting Kit lifted her spirits in a way nothing else had recently. She and Roy used to take the kids to Indigo Bay each summer to see a cousin on Roy's side of the family, play in the waves and take a break from the Texas heat and life on the ranch. It had been good for them all, and she hadn't been back in years—not since his cousin Danny, who took over the ranch during their vacation—had passed away.

"To visit the Wylders?" His expression had grown stormy.

"My friend Kittim Lane still lives there."

"You know Roy is happily remarried."

"And you know my life is officially none of your business." Maria said, standing up. She resented the implication she was going to Indigo Bay to stir something up between Sophia and Roy by visiting Roy's family. As far as she was concerned, Sophia could keep Roy.

Fiona arrived with the peppermint tea, her jaw dropping as she overheard Maria's words.

"Put it on my tab, please."

Fiona nodded quickly, but Maria knew the untouched tea would never show up on her running tally.

"Merry Christmas," Maria said softly. She strode to the door, hoping her invitation to Indigo Bay was still open.

"HANG ON. I WANT TO GET A MUFFIN," MARIA SAID, REACHING for her son Brant's arm as he drove past the Longhorn Diner.

"They have muffins at the airport," he protested, checking his watch. With a frown, he made a U-turn in the middle of Main Street and parked in front of the diner.

"The diner has the best bran muffins." If she was going to sit on a plane for over four hours, she wanted something good to snack on.

"Better than yours?"

"Yes, and Fiona won't share their recipe. They're that perfect blend. Not so dry you feel like you're eating sawdust," she said, undoing her seat belt, "and not so moist it's oily."

"You make bran muffins sound so appealing."

"It's a skill." She grinned and slipped out of his fully equipped veterinarian pickup truck.

"Like dodging Uncle Henry's Christmas party. How did everyone get out of going except me?"

"It never occurred to you because you're the best one out of all of us." Due to her week-long Indigo Bay trip, she would miss tonight's party. Maria gestured toward the restaurant. "Want anything?"

"Nope, I'm good, thanks." Brant held up his insulated travel mug and took a sip of coffee. April MacFarlane had a matching one, and Maria glanced at her son. April had grown up along with the boys, while her dad had worked as their ranch hand. April was a Wylder as far as the family was concerned, and they were all there for her now as she was going through a divorce.

Her marriage had been on the rocks practically from the moment she and Heath had uttered "I do." But sometimes Maria wondered if Brant had had anything to do with its rockiness. He was a good friend to April, and as his mother, Maria was proud of him and trusted him to do the right thing. Yet she couldn't help but wonder if some of April's problems had to do with Brant always being around to support her and be the friend her husband couldn't seem to be.

Shaking off those thoughts, Maria hurried into the diner, then tracked down Fiona at the back counter.

"You're off?" her friend asked, looking up with a smile. She shifted, sending the white fringe on her pink Western blouse swinging.

"Yes. And I need a muffin to go."

"You got it. Anything else?" Fiona handed her an already-wrapped bran muffin. "Pack your sunscreen?"

"And a hat."

"Where are you going?" asked a familiar, smooth male voice, sending tremors down Maria's spine.

She ran her fingers through the hair at the nape of her neck, ensuring tendrils hadn't escaped the loose bun. She fought the smile that always seemed to appear when Clint Walker was around.

Maria turned to face him. He was fit for being fifty-nine, his shoulders broad and strong. No doubt those muscles came from having to work rusted old bolts off the wrecks people called vehicles out here in Texas Hill Country.

"Indigo Bay. Kittim Lane asked me to come help with a fundraiser they're putting on for a local animal shelter."

"Barks and Bows?"

"How do you know?" she asked in surprise, handing Fiona her debit card. "Can I clear my tab, too, please?"

"Not coming back for a while?" her friend teased.

Clint took a more careful look at Maria, who blushed and said, "What?" She felt inexplicably guilty. "I clear it every week."

"My friend Jeff Brewster and I were talking about restoring an old scooter for the auction."

"For the Indigo Bay gala?" she asked, feeling as though the world was a little too small at the moment for this to be purely coincidental.

Clint nodded.

"And are you going?" she asked.

The prospect of seeing Clint away from Sweetheart

Creek thrilled her. But another part of her was scared of the thought of the two of them being free of everything that held them in their respective roles here in town.

"Brewster's been working on it alone, as I haven't been able to get away to help. I'm fixin' to take an extra long Christmas break and head out there. I haven't had a vacation in a long time."

"You should go," Maria said, starting to slip past him, and trying to avoid inhaling his wonderfully familiar scent of Old Spice and motor oil. "It's supposed to be a great event." She gave a confirming nod. "For a good cause."

Clint turned as she went by, and his slow, kind smile made her heart flutter. "Maybe I will," he said slowly.

Maria nodded again and tried to stop herself from scooting out the door, panicked that Clint might indeed show up in Indigo Bay. And that the real reason he did so might be because of her.

Maria inhaled the salty ocean air, absorbing the soothing vista of sea-green waves and the feel of sugary sand underfoot. She'd arrived in Indigo Bay last night and had slept in this morning, gone out for brunch, then spent a leisurely Sunday afternoon catching up with Kit on her condo's deck. Now they were walking the beach.

"I'm so glad you invited me to come out here," Maria said to Kittim. Her friend's heritage extended from the Middle East, and as a result she had gorgeous glossy black hair, beautiful brown eyes and a carriage and presence that always made Maria think of a princess. She was all the things Maria was not, and yet Kit somehow made her feel strong and as though her functional build was a foundation that could weather any storm.

"And I'm so glad you came," her friend said, brushing back a strand of hair that kept blowing across her face. It had a streak of white that hadn't been there the last time they'd visited, and was just another indicator of time passing. Kit bumped her hip against Maria's and wrapped her hand around her arm, giving it a squeeze. The affectionate gesture caused Maria's eyes to fill with tears.

When she sniffed, Kit drew back to look at her. "What's wrong?"

"I think it's been too long since I've had a hug." Maria swiped at her eyes, unsure where the sudden bout of emotion had come from. She wasn't like this.

"Aw, honey." Kittim pulled her into a tender embrace. "You're always so strong, and I'm sure everyone has leaned on you this past year. But who's been there for you?"

"I have friends like Fiona, of course," she answered. But Fiona had been going through her own hardships since her husband's accident. It had been several years now, but he wasn't doing well emotionally, his disabled status impacting him and their marriage more than his inability to walk.

And there was Clint. He'd been a wonderful friend, taking care of her car, making her laugh, bringing her a cup of coffee when she was volunteering around town. Little things to make her feel there was someone who noticed and cared, someone who had her back even though she was doing fine.

But she worried he wanted more than she could give, and as a result, accepted his small tokens with hesitance.

"Of course you have dear Fiona, but I'm sure you've had to put on a brave front even with her." They continued walking, Kit's arm hooked through Maria's. "I'm glad you got away for a few days so you can focus on the simple things." She gestured to the ocean, where some brave souls were playing in the waves, even in December. "And what's better than a beach walk?"

"Are you sure you don't want to move back to Texas with me?" Maria asked with a laugh.

"Are you sure you don't want to move to Indigo Bay? We have beautiful weather all year long."

"So do we."

"Your part of Texas doesn't have the ocean, and it gets too hot to breathe in the summer."

"If we're splitting hairs, Hill Country isn't the hottest part of the state."

"And your boys are still there. You can't leave, especially since Myles and Levi have finally found love. The other three will follow, now that they've seen the waters aren't shark infested. Soon there might be grandbabies, and you'll want to be there for that."

She would. Retirement hadn't proved to be the golden ticket. Maria had discovered during her months in town that she was a rancher, born and bred, and it wasn't something she could remove from her bloodstream. And maybe being a grandmother would fit her beautifully.

"I have to run out and meet the mayor at Sweet Caroline's about the shelter's gala. I'm the project's treasurer." Kit gave a wry smile. As an accountant, she was the treasurer for just about everything she volunteered for. "Did you ever meet Amanda Strickland?" Maria shook her head. "She's a great mayor. She does it all while balancing her own architectural firm. You'd like her. Do you want to continue your walk and meet me at Sweet Caroline's for supper in an hour?"

"Sure." Maria recalled the small cafe from years before. "It's still in the same place?"

"It is. Look for the blue awning if you get lost."

"Are you sure I won't interrupt anything?"

"You showing up will ensure the meeting doesn't go on for ages. Or lead to murder, if Miss Lucille Sanderson shows up and horns in. She's really nosing her way into this project." Her friend smiled wickedly before she peeled off to head across the sand toward town.

Maria continued to walk the beach, memories of Miss Lucille coming to mind. She'd all but run the town eons ago, and it wasn't difficult to believe she still had her nose in everyone's business.

Gulls circled above as Maria stopped to pick up a fragment of shell. It was smooth from the sand and waves, and she wondered how long it took for shells to wear down. Likely like life, a little at a time.

She began walking again, increasing her pace. The burn in her thighs and calves from the effort of staying balanced in the loose sand reminded her of all the things she'd neglected over the past year.

Back home, whenever she tried to go for a walk, she was stopped by people thinking her vehicle had broken down and she needed a ride. It was lovely, but it didn't help trim her hips or increase her cardiovascular fitness.

Soon Indigo Bay's public beach ended and homes appeared along the shore. Maria stuck close to the water, avoiding the private beaches so she wouldn't trespass. She'd made it past the first home, a stately renovated old mansion, when she heard her name on the ocean breeze.

The voice was awfully familiar and she turned toward the sound, her heart lifting. "Clint?"

He had come to Indigo Bay. And now, on her second day, they were already bumping into each other? How could that be a coincidence?

"I was wondering if I'd see you." Clint came across the sand wearing uncharacteristically bright surfing shorts. He also had on a rash guard shirt, and his shaggy graying hair was wet and tousled. He looked handsome. Healthy. Happy. And different from the quiet mechanic she knew back home.

"What on earth are you doing?" she asked, taking him in with a lingering second glance. He'd just come from the water, a short, wide board under his arm.

"Oh," he said, shoving a hand through his dripping hair. "I was learning to boogie board. The waves aren't that big, so it was about perfect for an old guy like me." There was that happy grin again.

"You're not that old."

"I'll feel old tomorrow when these muscles tell me I'm not twenty-three anymore."

"When did you get here?"

"A few hours ago."

"And you're already hitting the beach? I thought you had a moped to revamp?"

"Brewster's busy in his custom motorcycle shop, finishing up some Christmas orders. We'll work on the scooter this evening. Or at least that's the plan. I'm staying at his wife's B&B right here." Clint tipped his head toward the freshly painted mansion behind them. "Want to come in for a drink?"

Maria had never stayed in a bed-and-breakfast, but suspected inviting guests in for a drink wasn't standard practice.

"Sonja puts out sweet tea and snacks in the afternoon. There's a wonderful living room that guests are welcome to enjoy."

"It sounds lovely."

"And because I'm a family friend, I also have access to the liquor cabinet. So if you want something a little stronger than tea, just let me know." He gave her a devilish smile that took her by surprise. "I used to be a bartender in college."

"Really?"

"Yup."

The breeze was playing with Maria's shoulder-length hair and she pushed it off her face, wishing she had thought to wear a hat.

"Want to come in?"

The invitation felt as though it was for more than just a drink. It was an invitation into his life, into something new.

Into something she hadn't had since high school, when she'd started dating Roy.

That had been so long ago, she didn't believe she could do something like that again. New relationships took so much time and fuss. And anyway, how would their lives ever fit together?

Maria checked her watch, relieved to find it was time to head back and meet Kit. She gave Clint a regretful smile. "Sorry, I'm meeting Kittim for dinner soon."

"You're staying with Kit?" Clint asked.

She nodded.

"Is she working this week?"

Maria nodded again. "She runs an accounting firm."

"Maybe we could go out for coffee or something tomorrow while our hosts are tied up at work."

Maria knew from her stint as a retired woman that she was likely to go stir-crazy by tomorrow afternoon. But she also wasn't sure if Clint was inviting her out on a date. He'd been playing it cool back home, and right now he wasn't acting like a man who had followed her all this way. But still. Coincidence? She thought not.

"I'll call you if I have free time," she said, hoping to curb any false hope that she might inadvertently build by saying yes. She pointed to the mansion. "What's this place called?"

"Morrison Mansion Bed and Breakfast. But you can just text me. You still have my number?" The way he said it was flirty, and Maria paused, uncertain how to react to this new version of Clint. He was fun and free, and presenting himself like a very tempting distraction.

Not that she wanted to go home with a boyfriend. At her age! That was such a ridiculous idea. She had a ranch to help out on, no time for frivolity like some whimsical twenty-year-old.

But she was also curious about this newly revealed side of Clint.

Pulse thrumming, she turned into the wind, calling over her shoulder as she walked away, "I'll text you in the morning."

THE WOMAN BEHIND THE GLASSED-IN DESSERT COUNTER AT Sweet Caroline's had short brown hair and a warm smile. If Maria's memory was as good as she thought it might be, this was the owner, Caroline, now in her early fifties.

"I'm having that for dessert," Kittim announced, pointing to a slice of key lime pie nestled among sprigs of holly and mistletoe.

"Aren't we having supper?" Maria asked. The small cafe smelled of cinnamon, coffee and something sweet. Some of her favorite fragrances. The place was warm and bustling, nearly every table filled.

"We are, but we need to select our dessert first so we know how much to order for our first course."

The woman behind the counter grinned. "I like the way you think."

"Strategic," Maria murmured in approval.

"You remember Maria Wylder?" Kit asked Caroline. "She used to vacation here with her family years ago."

"I don't expect you to," Maria said, "but I sure recall your cinnamon rolls."

"Thank you." Caroline studied her thoughtfully. "Texas, right? Big family of boys?"

Maria nodded. "You have an excellent memory."

"Your Texas accent helped me out."

"It follows me wherever I go."

"Nick was here last summer. He's one of yours, isn't he?"

"My nephew."

"How's he doing?"

"Well, he and Polly are working together on my niece Alexa's ranch back in Texas. They seem happy." The duo had rekindled their old flame while saving Roy and Sophia's wedding here in June.

"Oh, I remember Alexa. She was another good one. Smart and sweet. Deadly combo. She was putting on a Christmas wedding—no, a vow renewal and reception for Luke Cohen and Emma Carrington, if I recall correctly?"

"She was." And had fallen in love with her boss, Cash Campbell, while doing so. It was lucky Maria wasn't here for anything wedding-related, seeing as two of her family members had fallen in love here while doing so.

Someone joined the line behind Maria and Kit, and Caroline got down to business, "So what would you like for your first course? Have you decided?"

They settled on two specials, then selected a table near the window, Caroline promising to bring out their meals when they were ready.

"How was your afternoon?" Kit asked Maria.

"Good. I went as far as the Morrison Mansion B&B. My legs have that wonderful feeling you get when you've pushed them a little."

"You seem pleased," Kittim said, a small smile toying with her lips as though aware Maria was holding back a secret.

"And I bumped into someone from back home," Maria blurted, wanting to talk about Clint. She would call Fiona, but worried that her friend might inadvertently start some gossip, or expect Maria to engage in something she wasn't ready for. Namely a relationship.

"Really? Who?"

"Clint Walker. He's my mechanic." She felt a blush heat her cheeks and a wash of possessiveness by claiming him as hers. Technically, he *was* her mechanic, but several hundred other people's, too.

"And he's cute," Kittim stated.

"You know him?"

"I can tell by your expression."

Maria looked out the window, watching a woman walk down the sidewalk with purpose, her little white dog trotting alongside. "He seems different here. More relaxed. Youthful." She gave her head a shake. A youthful fifty-nine-year-old was good, but not if he was being a daredevil.

But since when was boogie boarding classified as a daredevil activity? She used to take part in the rodeo circuit, and knew what risk-taking looked like. Watching a cowboy try to stay atop a fifteen-hundred-pound angry bull for eight seconds, for example. Was she looking for excuses to disregard Clint, or had she aged beyond her years?

Probably both.

"Are you interested?" Kit asked.

"I can't imagine adding a man to my life at this stage. It's too complicated. We're almost sixty, and I have the boys and the ranch. Carmichael isn't getting any younger, either."

"Your father-in-law?"

She nodded. "He's still out on the ranch." She added with a half laugh, "Levi, Myles and Brant are home, too." All the more reason it would be ridiculous to add a new man to her life.

"That's too much testosterone for me."

"Don't forget the two hired hands who live on the next section of land and come by for some meals."

Kittim just shook her head, then rested her chin on her hands.

"Clint was hinting we should do something tomorrow, and I basically said yes. But I don't know... What if he wants more than I do?"

"So you don't like him that much, then? Or just not romantically?"

Caroline came to their table with two plates. "No second chance for us older gals?" She gave them an apologetic look. "Sorry, I overheard the last bit. And I totally understand. I've been single for so long I figure what's the use in trying?" She put down their meals. "Then again, if Tom Selleck came in here… Or that cowboy with that wonderful mustache and gravelly deep voice. What's his name again?"

"Sam Elliott," Kit and Maria said in unison.

The trio went silent for a moment, as though in contemplation about how their lives might change if the handsome silver fox walked in and asked them out.

"He might be worth upsetting my routines," Caroline said with a wink.

"Maria got divorced this year. Her husband's remarried."

"Men move fast," Maria said.

Caroline squeezed Maria's shoulder in support. "I'm sorry, honey. Divorces are hard. Even harder at our age. I hope you're doing all right. Financially and whatnot."

"We both moved off the ranch, but I moved a tiny home onto the property and live there now. So all is as it should be." Her smile didn't feel convincing, and she couldn't figure out why. She should be happy. She was right back where she'd started. And this time with one less person to please. She rarely even missed Roy, causing her to realize just how much they'd drifted apart over the years.

When she'd returned to the ranch, even Carmichael had been happy. The old cowboy had smiled and almost hugged her.

It felt right being home again.

"Good for you," Caroline said. "Don't let him kick you out of your own home and life."

"I was no good as a town girl," Maria said, waving her

hand. "I'm glad the ranch was still there, and the boys welcomed me back."

"Of course they did," Kit said. She let out a quick laugh. "They needed their cook and maid."

"They've grown up a lot." And true, she had stepped back into the kitchen, but she didn't mind cooking for the group of them. It was what she'd done for a long time.

"I'll bet you also moved right back into the caretaker role."

"I am their mother."

Caroline murmured a sound of understanding.

"I think it's time to work on yourself."

"I'm fine," Maria said.

"I meant," Kit said, her tone soothing, "take some time for yourself and rediscover what makes you smile rather than work, work, work."

"I like the ranch."

"And it's work."

"I just spent six months living in town and reconnecting with myself."

"Did you? You said you were bored."

"I was."

"Then you were doing it wrong. You're supposed to find joy."

"I have joy."

"Does the ranch bring you joy?"

"It brings me purpose."

"But no joy?"

Maria heaved an impatient sigh.

"It sounds like life put you through the ringer," Caroline said sympathetically.

"She had her trust and her heart broken," Kit said. "And now it's time for her to celebrate herself."

"*Treat* yourself," Caroline said with a nod.

"Enjoy the freedom."

"Do the unexpected! Throw your arms in the air from the front seat of a convertible," Caroline said enthusiastically.

"Only if it won't throw your back out," Kit cautioned, and Maria couldn't help but chuckle. "And your seat belt is done up. By the way," she added, "do you still have that Mustang?"

"It wasn't a convertible. And I doubt it still runs."

"That's too bad."

"Standing up in a moving vehicle would be asking for trouble," Caroline agreed. "You want to live wild and free, but you also don't want to become a statistic."

Maria giggled.

"I say what happens in Indigo Bay stays in Indigo Bay!" Kit declared, catching glances from nearby tables.

Caroline's eyebrows shot up before she turned her attention back to Maria, her lips twitching with amusement. "Well, then. That sounds like permission to go live a little. Have some fun. Work on yourself, and if there's a handsome man interested in you, explore that avenue."

Maria shook her head, her feather earrings tickling her neck. "I'm here for a small break and that's all."

"She doesn't love him," Kit said, somewhat tragically, to Caroline. "He's from Sweetheart Creek, too." The gleam in her gaze turned slightly wicked. "I think he followed her here. And she thinks he's cute. But she's scared."

"He didn't follow me. He has a friend here, and they're working on a project for the gala. And I'm not scared."

"Have they been on a date?" Caroline whispered to Kit, as though Maria wasn't sitting right there, looking at her chicken potpie as it cooled.

"Not yet," Kit said.

"And not going to," Maria stated.

"Then of course she doesn't love him yet," Caroline continued, ignoring her. "She hasn't had a chance to fall. You don't fall in love without a date. He needs a chance to prove himself to her and show her there's more to life than her ex-husband."

"Preach it, girl!" Kit said, and they both turned back to Maria.

"No," she said, her head already shaking. "No."

Although discovering more than Roy was a bit intriguing. They'd married when she was twenty and she hadn't, technically, dated anyone but him. At least not seriously, seeing as her first boyfriend had been awful. All handsy and crushing her self-esteem with his comments and thoughts on how she should behave around him. She shuddered. No wonder Roy had seemed so amazing. And he had been, too.

But years of running the ranch together, falling into bed not out of passion but exhaustion from raising five boys and running their own business had sent them down separate roads and ultimately, apart.

"Go on the date," Caroline suggested.

"He hasn't asked me on a date," Maria said. Because she'd closed that door so fast he hadn't had a chance. Because he would have otherwise, wouldn't he?

"He wants to do something with you tomorrow," Kit pointed out. "And I'm going to be working all day."

"Sounds like the perfect time for the two of you to go on a date," Caroline said with a smile.

"Can we not call it that?" Maria said, dropping her head in her hands.

"Fine. How about calling it an exploratory expedition?" Kit giggled.

Amused at her friend's persistence, Maria rolled her eyes. "And what if I fall in love with this man? Then what will I do when we return to Sweetheart Creek? My boys will freak out. And I can't very well have him move onto my ex-husband's family ranch."

"Why not?" Caroline asked. "Your ex doesn't live there.

You do. And if you live on that ranch, I'm betting you're putting effort into it. I believe labor ownership is real."

"So do I," chimed in a waitress who was walking by, her arm stacked with plates.

"There are exceptions to labor equaling ownership!" Caroline teased, giving her employee a good-natured smile, which was returned.

Maria thought about her tiny home located in the yard of the Sweet Meadows Ranch. She had her own space away from the boys. Maybe that would make it less weird if she started dating.

What was she thinking? She wasn't looking to replace Roy. She was happy being single.

"I love that you're already thinking about living with this man." Kit said with a sly smile.

"I'm just problem solving. There are a lot of implications to dating again. The boys freaked out when they thought Clint was interested in me."

"Your sons noticed his interest?" Kit leaned forward.

"He's helpful and kind," Maria insisted, her cheeks heating. "He does little things for me and my car. My boys are busy, and he knows that."

The two women shared a knowing smile, and Caroline said, "Your suppers are getting cold. I'll let the two of you continue your chat." She gave Maria's shoulder a friendly squeeze. "Let me know if you need any Indigo Bay date ideas."

Maria huffed.

"Quit thinking about the future and just enjoy each day," Kit recommended. "If you fall in love you fall in love. If you don't, then no worries, right?"

"Sweetheart Creek is a small town." Maria had felt the sting of everyone knowing her and Roy's business, and she knew it was impossible to isolate herself from her ex. Every time she went anywhere it felt as though she was thrown against that constant pain once again. She didn't want a repeat. "Clint is the only mechanic, and my car is nearly a decade old."

"That's a weak excuse."

"It's true! Where would I go?"

"Date him. If things go south, buy yourself a brand-new car guaranteed not to break down."

Maria thought Clint's small moped—correction: scooter, because apparently there was a difference when talking to gearheads—was cute. That morning she'd taken a deep breath and texted him to see if he wanted to meet up for lunch.

Not because she was looking for a date, but because her curiosity had basically strong-armed her into it. Besides, she had nothing better to do and why not spend time with someone who made her feel good? Wasn't that the purpose of a vacation? Feeling good?

Now she was out behind the Morrison Mansion contemplating an old scooter with flaking paint. It didn't look like much, but it purred like her old car had after Clint had given it his magical touch. She wondered what else he could make purr.

"What do you think?" he asked his friend Jeff as he wiped his hands on a grease-stained rag. They stepped back and contemplated the machine.

The scooter was low to the ground, with a flat front that served as a bug and wind guard. It had handlebars similar to a bicycle, one giant headlight, no windshield and a padded seat with a smaller one behind. The floorboards were ample, giving the driver what looked like a fairly comfortable ride when the seats weren't worn to tatters.

"I can't believe how smooth the engine sounds," Jeff said.

"It didn't need as much as we thought it might."

"First time that's happened," his friend said with a chuckle. "I think it's time for a test drive before we talk paint."

"Might want to borrow some cushions from my wicker chairs on the porch," Jeff's wife said wryly as she joined them, gesturing to the scooter's seats. She'd been showing some volunteers the B&B's ballroom, which they were going to decorate for the weekend's fundraising gala. One volunteer had followed her out.

As Jeff leaned close to give Sonja a kiss, the wind tousled her dark blond hair. The two had found love again in a second marriage, and it reminded Maria of Kit and Caroline's encouragement for herself. She almost laughed out loud. She wasn't about to find this. Just a glimpse told her this pair had something rare.

The other woman cleared her throat and a flash of exasperation danced across Sonja's face.

"I'm Miss Lucille with the Ashland Belle Society. I'm checking all the silent auction items for their income potential for the shelter. Your little motorbike idea is very last-minute." She straightened her spine, nose high.

Miss Lucille Sanderson did still exist, almost exactly as Maria remembered her. Slender, impeccably dressed and snooty as could be. As her father used to say, only the good die young.

Introductions were made between Clint, Maria and Miss Lucille—who didn't remember the ol' cowgirl from the west. Naturally.

"She wants to see the scooter," Sonja said apologetically.

Clint and Jeff both swept an arm out to showcase the machine, which instantly sputtered and stalled, as though in protest of Lucille's appraisal.

"It's… disreputable," she declared with a sniff.

"The throttle probably needs adjusting," Clint said, crouching to look at the machine.

"Did you change the fuel filter?" Jeff asked.

Clint nodded.

"I trust this is not the scooter you're thinking of donating to the fundraiser." Miss Lucille hugged her big purse closer and a fluffy white head popped out of it and gave a small yip of disapproval. "Hush, Princess. I know. This is foolishness, but it can't be helped."

"It's not finished," Jeff said, his tone flat.

"We have a verified movie star coming, you know. Eric Slade. We must put our best foot forward." She eyed the scooter with disdain.

"It'll be looking so fresh, Miss Lucille, we'll even have you bidding on it," Clint joked.

"I doubt that. A woman of my means doesn't ride in anything with less than four wheels."

Maria swallowed a smile, then almost choked on a bubble of laughter when she saw Clint doing the same. She preferred doors, a roof and four solid wheels on the ground herself, but wasn't a snob about it.

"It was against my judgment," Miss Lucille continued, "to agree to holding the gala in such a small mansion. I fear nobody is taking this fundraiser seriously."

Sonja looked down, making it obvious she'd taken a bit of a browbeating from this woman over having her B&B as the hosting site.

"I assure you this scooter will raise quite a bit of money for the animal shelter," Clint said firmly, his mirth gone now.

"I've come all the way from Texas to work on it. As has my artist friend here." He clapped an arm around Maria, pulling her close. "Together we'll make this magnificent. I'll get it running impeccably and she'll make it shine, so unique it will be irresistible to those with deep pockets."

Maria's stomach flipped. "What?"

Clint nudged her. "Right, Maria?"

"No, I'm not…"

"Not going to share our big secret? You're so good about these things, but I have a feeling we can trust Miss Lucille. Please put her at ease and reassure her about our fabulous plan."

Maria's gaze darted to the woman's. Her eyes had narrowed, but she was listening.

"Retro is in," Maria blurted. "A robin's egg blue will make this scooter quite popular, especially in a beach town."

Clint grinned. "Perfect color! See? A few coats of robin's egg blue will have this thing winning the cutest-scooter-on-the-coast award."

Miss Lucille sniffed again. "That's hardly unique."

"Well, we can't tell you the entire plan…" Clint said.

Miss Lucille gave Sonja a hard look. "Don't let them disappoint me. This event reflects on our entire town. And if you want your B&B to be nominated for the Indigo Bay Best Business of the Year award, you'd better make sure everything goes perfectly."

"Hey, now…" Clint said, but his friend placed a hand on his arm, holding him back as Miss Lucille marched off.

"It sure will, Miss Lucille!" Jeff called after her, then added under his breath, "Don't worry about her. Her little society isn't even involved with the gala other than to offer a spa gift certificate as an auction item."

"Are you okay?" Maria asked Sonja, noting her bleak expression.

It lifted immediately. "Sorry, I was just imagining her gaining fifty pounds overnight." She patted her own curvy figure with a sly smile. "She's so vain she'd never step outside again and all our problems would be solved."

"She'd still have access to her telephone," Jeff muttered wryly. "Well, sorry to say, my lunch break is over." He turned to Clint. "Why don't you run it around this afternoon, tinker a bit more. See what else this baby might need before we paint it. If it's ready, we can start prepping it, otherwise we'll keep turning wrenches."

"Sounds good." Clint picked up a helmet sitting in the grass.

Well, so much for being a priority in Clint's world, Maria mused. Lunch had obviously been forgotten.

"I'm sure it'll raise a lot for the shelter," Sonja declared as she and Jeff headed toward a truck sporting a Seaside Cycles logo on the door. She kissed him goodbye and he drove back to work.

"Especially after our Texan artist dolls it up," Clint said, winking at Maria.

"I'm glad I'll be gone by the time the gala rolls around," she stated. "Then you'll have to deal with the fallout for it not being painted with a unique design." She patted his arm.

"Right, the boys' team has their state championship game on Friday. You're heading straight from here to Dallas?"

Maria nodded. "When do you head back?"

"Tuesday."

"Next week?" she asked.

"Tomorrow night."

"Tomorrow?" She'd assumed he would stay longer than two days.

"It's a tough time of year to ditch my responsibilities at the shop."

She looked at the scooter. It still obviously needed a lot of work, which meant she might not see as much of Clint as she'd feared. Now that the option was off the table, she felt disappointed.

"I know. Gearing up for Christmas is a lot of work." She still had some shopping to do and she hadn't even started her baking.

"I'm glad you're here," he said. "You need this time."

"That's what everyone keeps saying."

"It's true."

She focused on their earlier topic, not quite ready to discuss her need for away time. "So we're both reneging on your promise to make this scooter cute?"

"Not at all. You're an artist, right?" He started up the engine, then listened to it for a second.

"No."

He gave her a steady look and she frowned. She used to paint landscapes as a private hobby, but that was before having the boys. Which made it a lifetime ago. She likely didn't recall how to mix colors, and she'd definitely never painted a vehicle.

"I don't paint any longer."

"Ha! I knew it. You are an artist. I could sense it."

Maria rolled her eyes.

Clint pulled a screwdriver out of the toolbox in the grass and adjusted something on the machine, then revved it up a few more times before turning it off. Satisfied, he put the screwdriver back in the box. "Seriously, Maria. Will you help with the scooter?"

She shook her head.

"We can't leave Sonja and Jeff to the wolves. Well, wolf."

"*You* made the promise."

"Fine. So just help with the painting. You and I can put a few coats on this puppy." He tapped the machine's handlebars. "We don't have to paint any art on it. Just get it blue."

"I thought this was *his* project." She gestured toward the departing truck.

"I saw how busy he is with last-minute Christmas orders. Jeff says he'll do it, but I'm the one who convinced him. He'll either get to it around March when things slow down again, or else lose out on a paying job by working on it now."

"That's hardly fair."

"I know." Clint gave her a look that was best classified as puppy-dog eyes. "But I can't do it alone."

Great. She had no plans other than to help Kit with the odd fundraiser task, and now guilt would wrack her if she didn't step in and help Clint, too.

"I know nothing about painting a scooter."

"Just choose the right blue. I might get it wrong and then it won't win cutest scooter. Please?"

"Fine. I'll pick the color." That was easy and would take about five minutes, and might appease her sense of guilt. "But remember—not my project and not my responsibility."

He nodded solemnly and handed her a helmet.

"What's this for?"

"Aren't you coming with me?"

Maria gave the machine a dubious look. The pair of them on a scooter? The thing was barely big enough for one adult, let alone two. She'd have to cuddle so close she'd be like a second skin.

"We'll look like a circus act with both of us on that together."

"Are you calling me a clown?"

"Does the nose fit?"

"No, but the shoes do." He winked again and laughed.

"I used to be hesitant about motorcycles, too," Sonja said, walking by with a box labeled Fairy Lights that had been sitting outside a nearby shed. "But I found a driver I trust, and now I love going for a spin down the highway. You'd enjoy it."

"I don't think so." She was too big, and too old to do something so frivolously silly. "We're not a couple of teenagers."

"Why let them have all the fun?" Clint shot her a grin full of trouble and youth.

She was starting to worry about him. His lust for life seemed focused around forgetting his age, and they were approaching sixty. They didn't have time to deal with road rash, jellyfish stings or pulled muscles.

"I love that you have such a love for life," Maria said to Clint.

"But?"

"Sometimes people need to keep their feet on solid ground."

He had swung a leg over the scooter, but now dismounted and came over to her. "Everyone needs a little downtime." He was standing close. Not so near to be intimate, but enough that she noticed him in her personal space. He was acting as though he belonged there, and it felt like he did, too.

He gave her arm a gentle squeeze. "Let me take care of you. You're always taking care of others."

"I don't need to be taken care of."

"I know."

"Then why would you say that?"

"Because you look like you could use some fun."

"I have fun," she muttered, shaking off his hand. Great. Now she felt affronted, as well as miffed about their forgotten lunch plans. This was why you didn't get involved so late in life. Everyone had their own groove and couldn't be bothered to think of how to fit others into it.

"Maria, Maria…" he said gently. "Why not explore all this town has to offer?"

"On this thing?"

"We're not too old to try new stuff."

She felt the heat in his gaze as he said those words, as well as an increasing temptation to just let go and jump on the scooter. She used to have fun. Used to be bold and brave in ways she wasn't now. Now she was a rock. And where did rocks get you? Not on an adventure. Instead they weighed you down.

"I can't."

"Why not?"

"I'm responsible."

Clint laughed, his eyes crinkling. It had been a stupid thing to say, but having him laugh made her anger flare.

"So am I, sweetheart."

She rolled her shoulders, trying to sort out why the endearment was softening her. She didn't soften. Not for anyone. And not when she was ready to stand her ground.

"Do you trust me to take you out for a spin?"

"I came here for lunch."

He picked up a backpack she hadn't noticed. "Lunch."

She blinked. He'd packed food? That meant he hadn't forgotten. He'd planned. And the scooter, she suddenly realized, was part of that plan. A romantic, be-free-and-slightly-wild-without-standing-up-in-a-convertible plan. She didn't know whether to jump on the scooter or sit down and cry over his thoughtfulness. Or both.

"Let me take care of the petty things so you can savor a few moments of joy," he said. His tone reminded her of the one her veterinarian son, Brant, used when he was coaxing an animal into the clinic so he could help it.

"Like riding on the back of a scooter?" Was that joy?

"You won't know if you like it until you try."

She met his gaze, and that infuriating heat reared up like an unbroken horse again. It made her want to throw her arms around his neck and say yes, yes, yes!

"Life's short," he said, his voice deep and low and slightly hypnotizing. "Let's not waste another moment of it."

Lord have mercy, she was moments away from jumping onto the scooter and telling him to hit the gas.

Her eyes were still locked on his. His solid gaze was so trusting and sincere. She couldn't think of a single reason not to get on that machine, snuggle in close and let herself be free, if only for one simple, innocent afternoon.

"Clint?"

"Yeah?"

"Give me the helmet. Let's see how fast this thing can go with two old clowns shouting into the wind."

Scooters were not made for two people. At least not two adults who had filled out with age, life and children, or weren't ready to snuggle in close.

Still, it was remarkably pleasant, and Maria couldn't help but notice the firm muscles she clung to as she held Clint tight. He was driving down a beach road, the ocean at their side, the smell of salt and seaweed in the air. It was picturesque, with everything so blue and green despite it being December. The ocean, the sky. Then the pale browns of seagrass and sand. It made her want to take up painting again.

It hadn't helped, seeing all those wonderful paint chips at Seaside Cycles. They'd stopped by along the way to choose the right blue, in case Jeff couldn't mix it with what he had in stock.

A spark had ignited inside her as she viewed that wall of

paint colors. So many opportunities to brighten the world, one vehicle at a time. She'd walked straight to the color she'd envisioned for the scooter, but then had spent another twenty minutes admiring and dreaming about all the blues she hadn't chosen.

Clint slowed the machine, steering into a roadside lot. As he parked, she noticed the cove was popular with surfers, many of whom were riding the swells with an enviable ease. Clint placed his feet on the asphalt to support them as he removed his helmet.

He turned his head to look over his shoulder. They were close, way too close. Maria scrambled off the machine, removing her helmet, her buttocks aching from the worn seat.

"What do you think?" he asked, still sitting on the ancient scooter.

She slid the pack with their lunch off her back, then set it on the ground. "It got us here. Do you think it'll get us back again, too?" The scooter didn't look like much, but it had purred down the highway with the two of them on board. The trip had been slow, but pleasant, as Sonja had promised.

"Sure." Clint was casual, his moves fluid, belying his age.

"You give me such confidence." She'd said it tongue-in-cheek, but it was true. Clint had a way of settling her fears, anytime he was around.

"Glad to hear it. Want to climb that hill over there?" He slung the bag over his shoulder. "Looks like there's a bench with our name on it."

The breeze off the ocean was cool, like the air that had blown around them on the road, and with her body no longer pressed against Clint, Maria shivered. She tugged the zipper of her jacket a little higher and said, "Let's go."

The phone in her jacket pocket began to ring, and she answered it quickly, with an apology to Clint. "Hello?"

"Hey, Mom."

"Myles? Is everything okay?"

"Levi can't find the insurance papers for the truck, so I said I'd call."

"What happened to the truck?"

"Nothing. He's shopping around for a better deal."

"You can't leave the Ryder's insurance company!" They were like family. Everyone in Sweetheart Creek went to them. What were those boys up to? Changes were fine, but they were forgetting to take important things into account.

"The Ryders are selling."

"What? They are?"

"They just announced it today."

She hadn't heard a whisper about that. Maybe it was good the boys were so willing to take care of things these days. Levi was going to save her hours and headaches, pricing out a new insurance plan for the ranch and all of its vehicles and equipment.

"Okay. Tell him thanks. They're in the filing cabinet in the office."

"He already looked."

"It's under *V* for vehicles."

"Thanks."

She ended the call.

"Problems at home?"

She shook her head with a growing smile. "Levi's trying to save us some money. The Ryders are retiring, so he's shopping around for new insurance."

"They are?"

"Apparently."

"Makes sense. I'm pretty sure Joe Sr. was friends with Moses."

Maria laughed as they set off across the sand-littered parking lot, past an old Volkswagen van and a small pickup truck with a surfboard on its roof rack. As they neared an older Mustang, she pointed it out. "You know I have one of those in the machine shed? I used to think I was so cool in that." She smiled at the memories. The feelings were like those she'd just experienced on the scooter. The freedom and possibility. The ability to go anywhere. The right vehicle had always done that for her.

"What's it doing back there?" Clint asked.

She shrugged. "It's old, impractical."

"Still run?"

"I doubt it. It needed some work when I parked it."

"How long ago was that?"

"When the boys were small. You can't fit many rowdy kids in a Mustang. At least not that model, without someone kicking your arm and sending you into the ditch."

"Sounds like there's a story there."

She grimaced. "There's a story behind everything in life when you raise that many sons."

Clint chuckled. "Do you miss the car?"

Her smile grew again. "That car and I had some good times." She'd been driving it back when she and Roy would kiss at every stop sign and hold hands over the console. Her smile faded.

Some things were best left in the past.

They found a path that weaved between the dunes, leading up to the bench on the grassy hill. As they walked single file, the tall grasses whispered to them, spilling secrets she was unable to translate. She could see their destination, but the trail looked as though it was seldom used, while the one to the beach was much more heavily trafficked.

"Do you think there's a better path on the other side?" she asked, gesturing to a second parking lot to the south.

"Probably."

"Are we stuck?" She pointed to a sign requesting that visitors stay on the paths so as not to cause further erosion to the delicate plant life growing in the shifting sand. That meant no cutting across the grass to take the other path.

"Maybe."

"Should we double back and take the asphalt to the other parking lot to see?"

"You've been on the ranch too long, Maria." Clint gave her a kind smile. "We've got time to explore and take the wrong path." He tipped his head back, inhaling deeply.

Maria stared at him, trying to let go of the inner need to go, go, go. Get things done. Do them right the first time. Move on to the next task on the list. See who needs help. Get it done, get it done, get it done.

She needed to relax.

They continued upward, Maria's sandals sliding in the loose sand. Their path wound around to the ocean side of the hill, thin and barely there. She gasped in a steep spot when the shifting earth pulled her where gravity deigned. Clint turned, extending a quick hand to snag her before she tumbled to her hands and knees. His grip was warm and sure as he tugged her toward him.

For a moment she thought he was going to wrap her in his arms, but he stopped when she was a foot away, his gaze fixed on her lips. He slowly brought his eyes up to meet hers and she had that quickened-heartbeat sensation again.

She brushed off the nervous yet excited feeling of having a man look at her—really look at her—and marched past him. "I'll go first," she announced. She just hoped she didn't lose traction again and slide into him, her butt in the air.

Near the top, Maria found her confidence, her footsteps more sure as the trail zigzagged up to the summit. But wind and rain had eroded part of the dune, creating a sizeable gap between them and the top. Maria paused, unsure whether her newfound mountain goat skills included lifting her foot as high as her hip and then pulling her body along after it.

"Here," Clint said, moving past her. He hoisted himself onto the sketchy ledge with apparent ease. Once there, he knelt, reaching down to pull her up.

She hesitated a second, then put her hand in his, allowing him to help her. His wide smile told her he was glad to see her when she finally rose to her feet, their bodies a few inches apart.

"Hi," he whispered.

"Hi," she echoed, her own voice breathless. She wasn't sure if it was from the hike, or the proximity of his lovely dark eyes and that gaze that seemed to recognize parts of herself she'd forgotten existed. They'd become buried without notice, and she realized now that they needed dedicated attention and affection. Things that had always been in short supply over the past several years.

"Lovely hike, isn't it?" he asked casually.

She gave a small nod and continued on, her hand still locked in his. He made no move to release her, and she allowed the contact, curious where it might lead. The last time she'd held someone's hand, it had been little Kurt's—April MacFarlane's four-year-old—while crossing the street in Sweetheart Creek.

Hardly the same thing.

They took the last few steps to the bench, inhaling deeply, pleased with their ascent.

"We made it," she said.

"Feels good, doesn't it?"

"It does."

Clint was still smiling, an expression of hope that felt like more than she could support. She took her hand from his, making a point of illustrating a more gentle, well- trafficked path up to the bench. "See? There was another route."

"But ours was more fun."

"Well, I'm taking that one back down. Otherwise I'll end up sliding on my butt." Or falling into Clint's arms.

He gestured to the bench and said, "Shall we?"

The view was amazing, a fresh perspective that took her breath away. They could see the waves rolling and breaking, the sun dancing, the day so clear and beautiful.

"That wind is brisk," Clint said, as he pulled off the backpack and started taking out the food he'd brought.

"Refreshing." Just another thing awakening her and brushing away the cobwebs. Everything felt different in Indigo Bay. Her problems smaller, her worries receding. She hadn't realized how much she'd needed this change of scenery.

Was this the twilight after years of busyness? Was she at a point where she no longer had to worry over the negligible things, because she knew what genuine tragedy was? She'd learned to savor those small moments that could lift the heart, more than an expensive gift, a long trip or grandiose words.

"You look happy," Clint remarked, biting into one of the apples he'd packed.

"I am."

"Good. I'm glad." He looked like he wanted to brush back her hair when the wind whipped it across her cheek. He refrained, and she wasn't sure if she felt disappointment or a heightened anticipation of when he might reach out again, as he had when taking her hand.

They snacked in silence, Maria impressed and satisfied with his selection of food, from dark chocolate, chunks of specialty cheese, apples and nuts. It wasn't what she'd expected, and it thrilled her to eat something more than a practical but uninspired sandwich.

"The scooter ran well. Looks like I can paint it," Clint said.

"And replace the seat cushions."

He laughed. "And that."

Then it would be done, and he would have no reason to extend his stay. There'd be no unexpected moments to look forward to. Indigo Bay suddenly seemed a lot less exciting without the prospect of him being around.

"I'm free for dinner tomorrow. Want to go out somewhere with me before my flight? It would be an early supper, since I'll be leaving Charleston at nine."

"Like on a date?" Maria asked.

"If you'd like it to be."

She considered that idea for a second, before retorting quickly, "Would you?"

"I believe you know my intentions, Maria." His hand settled over hers.

Oh, there it was. He wasn't going to allow this to remain light and fun. He wanted something big and real.

"I've been admiring you for many years," Clint said, his fingers tracing hers.

"We hardly know each other." She took her hand away to busy herself with packing up the last of their lunch.

"I know plenty about you." When she gave him a look of disbelief, he continued, "I know you're patient and kind. You care about your community and friends. You're the glue that holds your family together, and you always put family first."

She nodded in agreement. That was what a dutiful ranching wife did. Farm and family first. His words could have described nearly every hardworking ranching woman in Texas.

She waved her hand. "Everyone knows that."

"Something more personal then?"

She dared him to cross the line, breathlessly waiting to hear what he would offer.

He hesitated, and she feared he couldn't think of something special and uniquely her. Had he stopped to think and realized that her entire existence could be filled by anyone?

With one arm along the back of the bench, Clint hitched himself closer. He pushed a piece of hair off her face, securing it behind her ear, then kept his hand there, cupping her cheek. His voice was low, his body blocking them off from the world. Now it was just the two of them, nobody else.

"I know that when you're feeling like your whole world is being rocked by a tsunami, you grow quiet. That's when you show your greatest strengths. That's when you step in and make things better for everyone else."

Oh, how she hoped he'd kiss her. Right here. Right now. Forget tomorrow or even five minutes from now. She wanted that kiss. She wanted to be recognized and held and cherished by this man who was bringing tears to her eyes.

He continued to lock her in his gaze, as solid and sure as the scooter that had brought them here. A swell of emotion caused her to blink and look out at the ocean, willing the wind to dry her eyes. Clint had dropped his hand, and he shifted to sit closer, hip to hip, his right arm still along the back of the bench behind her.

"I know you're used to being independent and alone."

"I'm not alone," she whispered, thinking of her boys. Their lives, their adventures, their projects, and now girlfriends for some of them.

"You're not used to having a man in your business."

"I was married for almost forty years," she said, her voice shaking.

"As much as I like Roy, I don't think he did good by you."

Maria bristled. If Clint thought slighting Roy was the way

to win her over, he was mistaken. She stood abruptly, wondering if she could figure out how to hail one of those ride shares back to town from here.

"You're not used to being noticed. Only when you're missing, when something isn't done."

"I'm appreciated," she said stiffly.

"I'm making you uncomfortable."

"Don't speak ill of my family and their intentions."

"I don't mean to, and I'm sorry if I'm coming off that way. You and Roy built an amazing family and raised five intelligent, hard-working boys who are great additions to our community. Not to mention the other kiddos you had a hand in raising, such as April."

"Then what's this about?"

"It's not about any of that. It's about you."

Her chest tightened, as did her hands. He was going to say things she didn't want to hear, make her face things she had put away in a trunk, intent on ignoring for the rest of her life.

"I'm too old and jaded to be wooed by you, Clint," she warned, reminding herself of that fact, as well. Despite that, she wanted to know what this man, who evidently had been watching and admiring her for years, thought about her.

"I'm not wooing you." Clint paused for a second, a quick frown wrinkling his brow before he said, "Okay, maybe I am. But telling you the truth is also being a friend. You know I admire you. And it's just honest-to-goodness truth that it's your time to flourish and focus on yourself."

"Clint…" she warned.

"I'm not fixin' to distract you with flowery prose and big promises or lies. I think you're an amazing woman. You know that already. What I think is this. You put others first and have for a good long time. Now it's time to put yourself first."

"Why? So I can spend that time with you instead of caring for my family and the ranch we depend upon?"

"No, so you can take some much-needed time to heal yourself so you can continue to help others."

"I'm fine, Clint. The boys are taking care of more and more each year."

"You know what I mean. It's not just the ranch stuff. People stuff, too."

She pushed the backpack into his arms and turned toward the wider path, preparing for her descent. "I appreciate your concern, but honestly, the divorce was a long time ago and everyone has moved on."

"You're a strong woman, but I think you took this trip for yourself."

She stopped at the top of the cliff and looked back. "Does it matter why I came here?"

"I think you could use someone standing behind you, supporting you so you can heal."

"There's nothing to heal!"

He paused for a second, absorbing her proclamation. "Then take a break. A vacation with energizing fun that revitalizes you, so you can keep on doing your best work."

She had to admit that sounded like what she needed.

"I think that someone like me could help you." Clint added.

She put her hands on her hips. "Okay, Prince Charming-who-leaves-tomorrow-night, why you?"

"Who else knows what you need? Who else knows the complications in your life, from your family to the ranch?"

"Plenty of people."

He raised an eyebrow, catching her in the lie. So, not that many. They had their own issues to deal with.

"Come on. Let's play."

She laughed. It was ludicrous, but oh so tempting. When

was the last time she'd let go of her worries and just played and laughed and enjoyed life? It had been a long time. Too long.

"I'm serious. Let's enjoy the full splendor of your golden years."

She held up a hand. "Please tell me you did not just say I'm in my golden years."

"They're golden, girl. Get over it. We're approaching sixty. Yes, sixty is the new fifty or forty or whatever they keep telling us. The fact is, you're rowing that big, heavy boat on your own." He had slung one of the backpack straps over his shoulder and now took both her hands in his, giving her an earnest look. "Wouldn't it be nice to have somebody help take the oars from time to time, so you could enjoy the small things more often?"

If Clint wasn't careful, he was going to be thoroughly kissed.

CHAPTER 4

"How are things at home?" Maria asked, holding the phone closer so she could video chat with her eldest son. By the looks of things Levi was in the Longhorn Diner on Main Street in Sweetheart Creek. That meant everything she said would be heard by at least one eavesdropper, then spread around town.

"The usual," Levi replied. "Ryan's too busy to do his share of chores, Myles is complaining because he already ate all the lasagna you froze for us, and Brant keeps showing up places with April while saying they're not a thing. So, you know. The usual."

"I've only been gone two days!" Maria exclaimed. "When Myles's metabolism slows down, he'll end up like a tractor. Big and slow moving."

"Speaking of tractors, Ryan can't get our old one running."

"What does he need it for?"

"He's trying to help Carly by running the cultivator behind it," Levi said, confirming Maria's suspicion that her son was trying to charm the new neighbor. Carly Clarke was starting an organic farm and had been turning up her garden plots by hand. She could definitely use mechanical help.

"Well, if you can't get that old thing going, you'd best buy a new one."

"Carly can't afford one," Levi's girlfriend interjected, joining the chat. "Hi, Maria!"

"Hi, Laura."

"I can make more lasagna for Myles if you'd like."

"If he finds out you know how, you'll be making it forever," Maria warned. "Myles is a bottomless pit."

"That's true." The voice was her friend Fiona's. Levi's camera turned and suddenly Maria was looking at her friend's chest, before he tipped the phone higher, giving her a view of her nostrils.

"Bad angle!" Fiona scolded, taking the device. She patted her teased hair while frowning at Levi, then faced forward again. "How are you, dear? Are you relaxin'? You're lookin' pretty."

"Thank you." Maria felt the telltale smile that had been semipermanent since that afternoon's picnic grow a little wider.

"Wait," Fiona gasped, as though hearing a particularly juicy bit of gossip. "Didn't Clint show up out there?"

"Clint went to Indigo Bay?" called a male voice, and before long Garfield was hanging over Fiona's shoulder. She shooed him off, saying she needed some space to breathe.

"I was hoping he could fix the tractor," Levi said in the background.

"Tell Carly to stop by the town's homesteading museum and get one of those horse-pulled cultivators. Maybe she can use that fat roan of Ryan's to pull it around her field. It's obviously no good for the rodeo work he was hoping to train it for."

Levi chuckled. "I think he saw the light and sold it."

Sometimes Ryan's independence and secret plans worked against him. Maria understood his desire for privacy, though. If you let the family or community know what you were up to, in short order everyone would be there, helpfully elbowing their way in. Everyone meant well, but did a poor job of minding their own business.

"Quit helping Maria change the subject," Fiona announced. "Did you two go on a date?"

Maria fumbled the phone. "No! No."

"A date?" Levi said, his voice rising in surprise.

"A date would be nice," Laura said from off-screen, no doubt trying to convince Maria's eldest to relax. The boys, grown men now, had faced several big changes over the past year and Maria knew it wouldn't be difficult to stir up the herd at this point.

"But you saw him?" Fiona pressed.

"We're friends. So, yes."

"Because William said he heard the two of you were going out for supper."

Maria groaned. Of course he'd overheard that. "It's just supper. Maybe. It's not a date, so don't you go spreading that around town."

"Clint's really nice," Laura said, her expression hopeful as she leaned in to be seen, letting Maria know she approved.

"He is," she agreed, appreciating the support. Maria hoped Laura and Levi would go the distance with their relationship. A city girl, she had turned out to be a quick learner out on the ranch, and Maria already couldn't imagine the place without her popping in to help here and there.

"So Ryan can sell the tractor?" Levi asked, taking the phone back from Fiona.

The waitress hushed him and the screen blurred as the phone changed hands once again, Fiona's face reappearing close to the camera. "We want to hear more about this date."

"It's not a date! And yes, someone can sell the tractor, but it won't be worth much if it doesn't run. Just like my old Mustang. But if you find a buyer for either one, take what they can give you in cash and run!"

Levi laughed.

"Maria?" Jackie Moorhouse, a friend of her sons, appeared on the screen. "Myles said you baked some buns for the football team's state championship potluck this weekend. I told the meal committee I'd bring them, but I don't know which ones you meant to contribute."

"All of them."

"There are at least ten dozen in the freezer."

"That's right. All for the potluck."

"You're amazing," Jackie said in awe, filling Maria with pride.

"Ryan says if we can get the tractor running," Levi continued, "its antique status would fetch a good price. Then we could buy something better."

"So he's selling off my equipment to give it away?" Maria asked, trying not to smile at the implications of what that would mean for Mr. Independent.

"Just to loan it out," Levi said. "I'd make sure of that."

"He's got it bad," Jackie said with a grin, jostling to be seen on the screen. "I took Carly to a football game, you know." She had a history of successful matchmaking at the games. If she had her sights on getting Ryan and Carly together, then it was pretty much a done deal as far as Maria was concerned.

"I know you did. Let's hope she sticks," Maria said. "I'm going for a walk. Tell Myles to eat some vegetables, and y'all do whatever you feel is best with the tractor." She let out a sigh, hoping Ryan didn't do something stupid in the name of love. Or whatever was developing over at the neighboring Lucky Horse Ranch.

"Oh," Levi blurted, before she could end the call, "and

Carmichael was wondering where you put the extra string of lights for the path. Brant said he'll put them up for you."

"Can't it wait?" Maria asked with another sigh. The guys were careful and meant well, but she wanted the lights strung evenly, and despite their best efforts, they didn't have much of an eye for design.

"Brant found a home for another one of Tootsie's kittens," Jackie announced from the side again.

"A good home, I hope." Maria's heart squeezed with worry. "The Fredericks wanted one, but their dog will kill it."

"No, he knows that."

Of course he did. He was a top-notch veterinarian and would ensure the cat found a safe home. She needed to let go of her worries. They weren't kids any longer. They were adults, perfectly capable of taking care of themselves and those around them.

"Enjoy your date with Clint!" Fiona called from somewhere in the background, no doubt alerting the whole town in the process. "Text me when he kisses you!"

"It's not a date! It's supper. Maybe. And there will be no kissing."

She went to hang up, but Levi interrupted her goodbyes with a quick, "I almost forgot. The accountant called. He needs some paperwork from last year's grant. He said you'd know about it."

"I'll get him the file when I return home."

Maria ended the chat before there could be more interruptions, then leaned back in her chair, exhausted. She missed Sweetheart Creek and being in the center of things, but not nearly enough to want to go home. Not yet.

Did she really deal with that much stuff each day? No wonder everyone kept telling her she needed a break.

She left Kittim's condo, enjoying the evening sunshine. It wouldn't be long before dusk settled in, bringing cooler temperatures, but at the moment it was perfect. Not too hot, not too cold.

After a few minutes of wandering, she found a giant Christmas tree set up in the downtown square.

"Hang an ornament on the tree on Christmas Eve and make a wish," a young woman said as Maria passed. She had a small stand with handmade ornaments for sale.

Maria continued a few more paces before the words sunk in. *Make a wish?*

She stopped walking, a wish immediately coming to mind. She turned, facing the tree and the person who had spoken.

"The tradition is if you make a wish when you hang your ornament here on Christmas Eve, it will come true. They light the tree at five o'clock that day, and supposedly that's when the magic begins to happen."

"The wishes have come true?"

She shrugged. "There's no risk in trying." Seeing Maria's hesitation, she came a little closer, saying in a quiet voice, "I made a wish and it came true. So did my sister."

Maria opened the change purse she kept in her jeans back pocket. "I'll buy one. How much are they?"

The woman gestured to her small display of different-sized ornaments, with prices to match. There were hand-painted lighthouses, animals, beach scenes, and a few quotes from poems she recognized. The artist had patience and a steady hand. It was a talent Maria had long ago ignored in herself. How had Clint known she was an artist? Had he merely guessed? And *was* she an artist? She didn't feel she could call herself one.

She lingered over the ornaments, finally choosing one that said Family Is Where the Heart Is.

She paid for it, then silently held the painted clamshell between her hands, breathing slowly as she faced the giant tree. She inhaled its pine scent mixing with the salty air around her. Overhead a gull cried, and she continued to breathe and hold the ornament as though transmitting her hopes, fears and dreams into it.

When she was ready, she made her wish, then reached up to hang the shell deep in the branches, where it would be safe. A small bird flew out from its hiding spot among the needles, and Maria squealed and laughed.

"It likes to do that to people," the woman said. "Why don't you wait until Christmas Eve to hang it, so your wish can come true? That's when everyone comes back with their ornament."

"I'll be home in Texas by then." And trying to figure out how to do Christmas with her boys *and* her ex. She wasn't looking forward to that. "Is it okay if I put my ornament on now?"

The woman shrugged. "There's no law against it."

But would her wish come true?

Probably not.

Her son Cole had been away from home for almost five years now. No cards, no emails. Nothing but silence.

Maria stepped back from the tree, worried that she'd jinxed her wish by not adhering to the town's tradition. Shoving her hands deep in the pockets of her sweatshirt, she headed toward the pier that stretched out over the ocean.

She was a block away when she spotted a man walking toward her, strolling along as though he had all the time in the world.

For a moment she thought her wish had already come true. But as the clouds above shifted, sending a stream of sunshine onto the man heading her way, she realized she hadn't conjured up her long-lost son, but Clint Walker.

With every step he took toward her with that warm smile upon his face, she realized her response actually resembled homesickness and longing. She missed Cole as only a mother could, but there was something about Clint that made her feel as though she'd been denied something equally important for far too long.

She wasn't sure what it was, but she vowed she would find out before he left Indigo Bay.

"MARIA," CLINT SAID WARMLY, CAUSING HER HEART TO LIFT AS he wrapped her in an embrace that snugged her briefly against him. He released her with a kiss on the cheek in a way that seemed European. At the last minute she almost gave in to the urge to turn her mouth to meet his.

"Are you Italian?" she asked. He had black hair and a complexion that always looked sun-kissed.

"I don't think so, but maybe," he said. "Are you?"

"Cherokee and Spanish, or so I've been told."

"That explains those beautiful cheekbones and deep brown eyes of yours." He gave her an appreciative look that sent a rush of heat through her. She wasn't used to being gazed at like that, and fought the temptation to encourage him to provide more details about just how gorgeous he found her.

"Are you putting the base coat on the scooter tonight?" she asked. They began to walk along the pier together, a few birds resting on the railings, heads tucked under their wings.

It felt natural bumping into Clint, walking and talking, assuming they'd spend time together. She had a feeling she'd miss him when he returned home tomorrow night.

"Brewster figures we can do it tonight after supper. I still think it would look good with some original art on it."

"Flames?"

Clint chortled. The scooter had been speedier than she'd

assumed, but not so much she felt flames fit its character. He pulled his phone from the back pocket of his jeans and began scrolling through pictures before showing her a close-up of a spot on the front wind guard.

They stopped walking, Clint's shoulder brushing hers. "We're thinking we could paint a little scene below the headlight."

"That could be nice."

"We just aren't sure what would look good and appeal to many." He put his phone away.

"You don't have much time to paint something like that." They were five days out from the gala, and Clint had only another twenty-four hours in Indigo Bay.

He shrugged. "That's Brewster's job. I'll help as much as I can, but bodywork's not my specialty."

"You should stay longer and help him."

"Yeah?"

She lifted a shoulder, trying to look casual. "Sure."

"Say I managed to take a few more days away from my shop..." His eyes lingered on her face. "What would a guy like me do around here for that long?"

"I'm sure you could think of something." She patted his arm and began walking again.

"You fly straight to Dallas on Friday morning?"

She nodded. Brant would pick her up at the Dallas airport on his way to the high school state championship game. She'd ride home to Sweetheart Creek with him afterward.

"So if I moved my flight, we'd have a few days to get into trouble?" Clint rubbed his hands together as if plotting something evil.

"I'm helping with gala prep."

"Oh?"

"I'm doing some running around and crafty stuff."

"You craft?"

She shook her head. "Not really."

"And that'll keep you busy all day, every day, until Friday?"

She smiled.

"It won't. You're going to be bored. You were bored during your retirement and the idea of being stuck alone all day with nothing to do has you breaking out in hives." He grabbed her arm and pushed up her sweatshirt sleeve, making her squeal. "Yup. As I suspected. Hives."

She checked her arm. Clear of any kind of rash. "No hives."

"I am hereby reporting for duty and will extend my stay to keep you healthy and safe from more hives."

She laughed.

"Hives are very serious business, Maria."

"You can't neglect your business because I might get bored, Clint!" She pressed a hand against his forearm and he crooked it, tucking her arm so it was hooked in his. She leaned against him slightly as they walked, and he did the same.

"If I stay will you paint something on the scooter for us?"

"Nope."

"Why not?"

"No time."

"That's not the actual issue."

Maria felt a jolt of surprise, at his mildly stated, but firm disagreement. She took a second look at Clint.

He seemed amused. "You're not used to people challenging you, hanging on your every word, spoken or unspoken." He had a teasing glint in his eyes and she narrowed her own.

"As a matter of fact, people don't mess with me."

He gave a long, deep bow. "Forgive me, my queen."

Some joggers turned to take a second look as they went past.

Maria laughed self-consciously. "Unbend your spine, you silly old man."

He placed a hand on his back and groaned. "I'm stuck!"

She squeezed his arm, her amusement becoming concern. "You are not."

He grinned and straightened. "Anyway, I thought we weren't old? Weren't in our golden years yet?"

"Do you remember everything I say?"

"Yes."

Well, that could be a problem. He was going to hold her to things she wasn't sure she was ready to be held to.

"How about this?" Clint asked, draping an arm across her shoulders as he led her toward a stand selling roasted nuts. She felt cozy and safe that way, the gesture natural. "You help with the scooter and I'll help with your crafty stuff. I'll see if I can stay all the way to Friday and we'll get into wonderful mischief and run away from home because the ocean keeps calling us."

She laughed.

"I'm serious."

"If you can help with crafty stuff, why can't you paint a scene on the scooter?"

He paid for a bag of warm nuts and offered her first dibs. "Probably because it'll look like it got splattered on there by a gifted elephant."

Maria laughed again, the image clear in her mind. "That might work, you know."

He frowned into the distance. "Weren't we going to have supper if we bumped into each other tonight?"

"This doesn't count?" She nudged the bag of nuts.

"Only if you add a corn dog from over there, and a coffee

from there." He pointed to other food stands. "But that's not—"

"Done deal."

"—what I had in mind."

"But it works for me. Doesn't it work for you?"

He was frowning, his wonderfully dark brown eyebrows knitted together.

"Loosen up, Clint. It'll be memorable. More so than some burger joint."

His gaze found hers, his brows relaxing as that warmth reentered his eyes. "Who are you? Where's Maria Wylder?"

"What?"

"You implied a hodgepodge meal would be more special than a sit-down dinner, and told me to loosen up."

"So?"

"So?" He looped his arm through hers again. "I like that you want to do special things with me."

"I've decided that a break is what I need, as well as some fun." She gave him a stern look. "Don't read into it."

"I happen to enjoy reading." He offered her more nuts. "And I like that you're taking some time for yourself."

He left it at that as they exited the pier, getting in line at the corn dog stand.

"My treat."

"Fine."

"What I was thinking with the scooter painting—since I'm no good at it—was that you would be our Picasso and I would be your minion. I'd bring you coffee and rub the tension from your shoulders."

"You seem to think I've said yes."

"Haven't you?"

"No."

"But didn't I just agree to move my flight for you, and you said you wanted to take some time for yourself?"

Maria paused. "Yeah, but..."

"I made a promise, Maria. I always keep them. Always."

She opened her mouth to protest, but couldn't find a suitable retort.

"Here's a sample of what my hands can do." Before she could utter a word, he had spun her around and was deftly kneading knots between her shoulder blades that she had long ago accepted as part of aging. But now, with Clint's fingers coaxing them to give up their tension, she wondered why she'd never asked a man to give her a back rub before.

When they reached the front of the line, the stand's Christmas lights blinking merrily, he dropped his hands from her back. She wasn't one to pout, but the absence of his touch nearly had her doing so.

"Painting? Back rubs? How can you say no?" He opened his wallet while saying to the man at the stand, "Two, please."

"What's in it for you?" she asked curiously.

"I get to spend time with a woman I've been intrigued with for years."

"Years?"

His dark brown eyes gazed straight into hers as he confirmed, "*Years.*"

Years.

"I'll think about it."

In fact, she was pretty sure she wouldn't be able to stop.

THE NEXT DAY, WHILE KITTIM WAS AT WORK, MARIA FINISHED dropping off last-minute Indigo Bay Animal Shelter adoption day flyers to the few stores in town that weren't yet sporting one in their window. The shelter's adoption drive would be held on the Tuesday following Saturday's fundraiser gala.

After delivering the final flyer, the last item on her to-do list, Maria propped her hands on her hips and studied the sky. A bit cloudy. Definitely a good day to be indoors, and the Indigo Bay retailers seemed to know it. Quite a few businesses were entertaining tourists with mini events such as cookie decorating at the bakery, chocolate making at the Indigo Bay Chocolate Emporium, and ornament painting at the jewelry store, Coastal Creations. Even Happy Paws, the pet store, was offering fifteen minutes of free pet-training tips. From a block away she could hear the dogs barking in joy at being all together under one roof.

Maria's ingrained habit of getting up at dawn to do chores on the ranch meant she'd already walked the beach.

So now what?

"I had a feeling if I wandered around town long enough I'd run into you," said a deep voice.

Maria turned to find Clint.

"Good morning," she said.

"Free for lunch?" He checked the black watch on his wrist.

"As a matter of fact, I am."

"Sweet Caroline's?"

"It was lined up out the door when I went by a few minutes ago. Caroline's giving away Christmas cookies today. I got mine earlier, but it looked as though half the town had turned out by now."

"How hungry are you?" Clint asked.

"Actually, not super hungry." It was still early for lunch. "How about you?"

"Let's go find something to do until Caroline's clears out."

"Sounds good."

As they strolled past the jewelry store, filled with locally made items, Clint stopped. They looked through the windows at the bustling front room. "What's going on here?"

A woman in a smock was about to close the door. "We're painting ornaments."

"Painting?" Clint's eyebrows rose, and he swiveled to look at Maria.

"There's another session following this one that's a bit more family-oriented and crafty."

"She's had enough of being crafty for one day, I think," Clint said, referring to Maria. "Painting is more up her alley."

"Would you like to join us?" the woman asked. "We have two empty spots left."

"Perfect. There are exactly two of us." He was already walking inside. Through the doorway Maria spied a throng of giggling women eyeing Clint as if he were candy.

Maria hustled after him, catching Clint at the cash register, already paying for them.

"Are you sure you want to paint?" she asked nervously.

"Worried you'll show me up and crush my delicate male ego?" He winked and picked up an ornament from the box on the counter, without considering the selection.

The woman behind the counter instructed them to choose red or white wine from the staffer pouring glasses at a table nearby.

"Wine, too? It's almost like a date." He nudged Maria, and she shook her head and smiled.

The woman with the wine lifted a bottle of red and a bottle of white, giving each a waggle.

"I like this town," Clint said. "Red for me." He turned to Maria, who held up two fingers to show she'd like the same.

"I think we only get one glass each," he said seriously.

There was a sparkle in his eyes that caused Maria to roll her own. "You're so silly."

"Come on, let's pick a spot to sit," he said, collecting their glasses after handing her his ornament to carry along with her own.

They found seats at one of the folding tables near the front windows. Clint handed her a glass, and she took a large sip, feeling a sudden bout of nerves.

What was she doing? Was Clint going to expect her to create something amazing? She'd never painted on glass before, and wasn't sure how the curved surface would affect whatever she attempted.

"Hello! Are you new to town?" an older woman with unnatural blond hair asked. She seemed to be looking down her nose, even though technically she wasn't. In her lap was a large purse with a small, fluffy white dog inside.

"Hello, Miss Lucille," Maria said.

"We've met?"

"At the Morrison Mansion Bed and Breakfast."

"Oh, yes. The two of you are working on the death trap. The gala and silent auction are only days away, you know." She eyed the glass of wine in Maria's hand, which was now half-empty. Then her gaze dropped to the ornaments on the table in front of Maria and Clint, as though she would be judging their painting ability.

"What an adorable dog," Clint said. "What's his name?"

"This is Princess," she said, bristling. "Her collar matches my shoes. And she is obviously a female!"

"My apologies," Clint said mildly.

"She's adorable," Maria stated politely.

"We coordinate every day. Hardly anyone notices," the woman sniffed.

"I'm Maria Wylder and this is Clint Walker," Maria said, feeling as though introductions should be made again.

"Taking your husband's last name is a sign of respect. It's the proper thing to do, you know."

"We're not married yet," Clint said smoothly. He leaned across Maria to shake the woman's hand, resting his left palm on Maria's shoulder blade and sending warmth through her body. "But I'm working on it." He gave the older woman a wink.

Miss Lucille bristled. "Are you a late bloomer or did you already leave your first wife?"

An involuntary gasp left Maria's lips, but Clint just smiled. "I'll have to tell you all about it later. But I'm here until Thursday night, then little elves are going to whisk me back to Texas."

The woman's expression grew stern and she turned away as their instructor began introducing herself.

"You moved your flight?" Maria felt a thrill zip through her.

He nodded as a woman on the other side of him gave in to giggles she'd been trying to stifle. When she regained control she whispered, "Sorry, my aunt can be a bit much." She gestured to Miss Lucille.

"Oh, did you want to sit beside her?" Clint shifted instantly, ready to move, but the woman shook her head, eyes wide.

"No, that's okay," she said too brightly. "I'm Maggie."

Clint and Maria whispered their own introductions while trying to simultaneously listen to the instructor. She was saying something about the kind of paint they'd be using and how long it would take to dry. Quite quickly, by the sound of things. That would make blending colors a trick and a half.

Miss Lucille gave a loud, harsh *"Shh!"* at the end of their introductions.

"Sorry!" both Maria and Clint chirped. Maria dived into her wineglass and noticed Clint did the same. When his eyes cut to hers over the rim of it the giggle that had been building inside her escaped, drawing another shushing sound from Miss Lucille. Maria shut her eyes, tightening her lips as she tried to hold back her laughter.

She could not look at Clint. Could not. She'd never stop laughing.

She looked.

His eyebrows danced, and she lost control, a loud bark of laughter startling the class.

"Sorry!"

"How much have you had?" Clint whispered, his shoulder pressing against hers as he checked out her wineglass.

She giggled, her face burning. "We should leave."

"No way. This is just getting good, girl."

"I'm hardly a girl."

"You're blushing like one."

"It's embarrassment."

"Would the two of you be quiet already?" Miss Lucille snapped. The woman in a sweater set across from her gave them a look of intense disapproval.

"Come sit over here," called a man from another table. He and his girlfriend shuffled their chairs to make room despite the crowd at their table.

Clint was up in a second, collecting their glasses in one hand, their chairs in the other. He hurried over, whispering, "Is this the fun table?" He hunched low as he set down their glasses.

Several people nodded, grins on their faces.

"Great." He pulled out Maria's chair and she sat, feeling both embarrassed by her outburst and full of energy. She wanted to be silly and to laugh at ridiculous things all day.

"How am I going to sit still for this?" she asked, staring at the glass ball in her hands.

"Drink more wine."

"I don't have any ideas for this ornament."

Clint reached over with a brush dipped in green paint and slashed a mark across it. She gasped. "Hey!"

"You have to make that work."

"What?"

"You have to keep the green stroke and work it into your design."

"I don't have a design."

He checked his watch, then the clock above the display cases of sea glass jewelry. "You have approximately fifty-six minutes to make one."

The room grew quiet as people contemplated what to paint, then chatter built once again until it filled the room.

Clint hunched over his ball, adding brushstroke after brushstroke. Maria couldn't think of a single thing to paint.

She pressed against him, trying to see what he was doing. He leaned away, body curved around his ornament. "Hey! Don't steal my ideas."

"I wasn't! I just wanted to see."

"Fifty-three minutes," he warned.

Maria sighed and contemplated the fist-sized ball. It had been so long since she'd held a brush she wasn't sure she recalled how to do it.

Eventually she began adding more green around Clint's mark, turning it into a palm tree. The room around her began to fade as she zeroed in on the smooth glass in her hand, the fine-bristled paintbrush and the colors that subtly changed depending on which tones neighbored them. She loved that about painting. Colors were flexible in how they could take on the tones of others. Kind of like people. When she hung out with Clint, she relaxed and laughed more. She liked that. She liked how hopeful and upbeat she felt. If she were a color, she'd be one of joy. Maybe a sunny yellow or a pink that popped.

She wondered how she made Clint feel. She turned to ask him, caught sight of his painting and burst out laughing.

"No?" He fought a smile, twisting his wrist so she had a better view of his completed ornament.

"It's charming."

He'd taken a stab at painting Santa Claus, the rounded ornament enunciating the size of Santa's belly. Proportionally, he had done quite a good job, the painting playful and endearing. A lot of the qualities she saw in Clint.

She looked at her own ornament. She had painted the beach she'd been walking each day. Uninspired. Too much brown. Too much green. Too much blue. Too boring. Too flat.

She had checked off all the appropriate "good painting" boxes when it came to proportion, color, tone, balance, adhering to the rule of thirds and all the rest of it she'd learned in art class. But her ornament lacked character. It lacked a story, originality and life. It was precise, the technique shaky but solid. Overall it was cliched and forgettable.

She set down the ball.

Clint was watching her.

Maria tried to catch sight of what others had painted, but most people had already set theirs in the cardboard holders and boxes for drying and taking home. Maria had been the last one still painting.

Miss Lucille didn't seem to have painted anything, but had been gossiping about the Ashland Belle Society and the upcoming gala as though she was in charge of it all.

Feeling an uncontrollable urge to correct her, Maria stood, saying to Clint, "Let's get out of here."

"What was wrong with your painting?" Clint asked as they left Coastal Creations. He had collected his ornament, having the mostly-dry ball carefully boxed and bagged. Maria had left hers behind, telling him she'd meet him outside.

"You didn't like it?" he asked, when she dug her hands into her sweatshirt pockets and walked faster.

"It was boring." And it represented everything she had been ignoring in her life until now. The worst part was that everyone else could see it. Roy had left her. Kit wanted her to loosen up, as did Clint and Fiona. Maria had been having a midlife crisis without even realizing it.

Clint hustled to keep up with her. "Boring?" he asked.

"Yup."

"Did you enjoy it?"

She picked up her pace.

"Hey, slow down."

Her steps faltered. "Have you ever taken a moment to look up after working hard all your life?"

"Sure."

"And then realized that none of it..." She gestured futilely, unable to find the right words to express how she felt. It had all been worth it. She had her boys, a thriving ranch that supported several generations. She knew her sons loved and appreciated her. She didn't have regrets. Not specifically.

But still, something was missing.

"None of it matters?" Clint offered, his features lined with concern. "Defines who you are?"

"This isn't a fill-in-the-blanks test."

"Talk to me. Just keep talking until it all makes sense."

Maria exhaled, trying to collect her thoughts. She didn't know what to think. What to say, or where to start.

"Who do you see when you look in the mirror?" Clint suggested. When she heaved an impatient sigh, he reached over to give her elbow a supportive squeeze. "Talk to me."

"I'm too task-focused. I take myself and my life too seriously."

She faced Clint for a long moment, as he studied her.

"Know what I see?" he asked, his voice gentle.

"Do I want to?" She wasn't in the mood for compliments.

"I see a woman who puts pressure on herself to achieve and hold things together. And maybe she's feeling a little lost because her place in the world doesn't feel as make-it-or-break-it any longer. Her family's grown up and fairly independent. A big slice of your identity was the boys, Maria. It makes sense that you're wondering where you fit in now that they're peering down the path toward starting their own families."

She felt her eyes dampen.

"Hey…" Clint pulled her into a tight hug that felt like everything she needed. "It's okay."

"I know."

"It's just time to change gears."

"But how?" She was still an important cog in the ranch's operations, and didn't want to give that up. But again, something was missing. Something felt overlooked.

"Like with the town library. I heard you helped Karen get the mental space to battle against Henry, who was standing in her way." Clint released her enough to look at her. "In the old days you would have been up all night baking your amazing squares to sell in a fundraiser. But we're old."

"Don't put me out to pasture!"

He chuckled, his gaze on her lips again, heat turning his brown eyes into depthless pools she wanted to explore.

"All I'm saying is that how we contribute is shifting. We have a novel kind of brawn now. It's time to let the next generation pull the weight while we sit on our mountaintop and wait for them to need our insights."

Maria laughed at the image of her sitting on a mountain like a wise old sage. Although she understood what he was saying. She used to run around baking and doing crazy amounts of labor for various fundraisers. This time, however, she'd stepped forward to advise and clear paths. It was still important work, and it was still support, just different. A different energy.

"It's our time to slow down and enjoy life. Don't you think?"

"But it's hard."

He smiled. "That's because you're amazing, and you're wired to take charge and get things done."

Maria rolled her eyes. "I'm boring. I painted the most boring scene on that ornament."

"You take any task given to you very seriously, and that's appreciated by everyone you work with. But you know what else I see?"

"Hmm?"

"This Maria Wylder chick can also turn around and tease someone else until they beg for mercy."

"I don't see anyone begging."

"I'm begging, Maria." His eyes had locked on her mouth. His voice lowered until it was barely above a whisper. "Trust me, I am begging."

Maria licked her lips, confused and unsure what to say or do. He had released her from the hug, but they were still standing close. Closer than friends would, but not so near they'd be mistaken for lovers.

"Can I kiss you?" He was the most serious she'd ever seen him. Even when, a few months back, he'd informed her she needed a new transmission in her car.

"You shouldn't have to ask that," she said, frustrated that he didn't feel he could be spontaneous with her. With some things, yes, such as picnics, scooter rides and ornament painting. But not with a kiss, the one thing that should be unplanned and from the heart.

Was this indicative of her entire problem? She'd lost the ability to relax and go with the flow?

Clint shuffled his feet closer to hers as his callused hands bracketed her face. The kiss was tender and sweet, tasting of gingerbread. He must have stopped at Sweet Caroline's for a cookie as well. He kissed her for a long moment, forcing the pre-Christmas foot traffic to weave around them.

"You left the painting class to come outside and do this on our streets?" said Miss Lucille with disdain. "Tourists," she muttered, and Maria couldn't help but giggle in Clint's arms.

"We sure did," he called after her.

As Maria pulled Clint in for another wet kiss, she thought maybe she was already learning to not take herself so seriously.

CHAPTER 5

*M*aria let herself and Clint into Kittim's condo, then closed the door and leaned against it, smiling. The energy surge from giggling like a teenager in the painting session had returned full force. She was brimming with unexpected joy and delight, as well as curiosity over what might come next.

"You're even more beautiful when you smile," Clint said, easing closer to cradle her face. He gave her a light kiss on the lips. While it was chaste, it held a heat that whispered of promise.

She smiled again, feeling ridiculous. Was this how Roy had felt when Sophia had paid attention to him? Renewed? Excited? Full of anticipation that there might be more to life yet to come?

No. No thinking about Roy under any circumstances.

She was here, away from home and everything that kept tying her to an identity that no longer served her. Things had changed, as Clint had so deftly pointed out. It was time she changed, too. Just a bit.

"Want a cup of tea?" she asked, slipping past Clint and

heading down the narrow hallway to the kitchen and living area. She pivoted, walking backward to watch him. He advanced with a smile, catching her in his arms to give her a kiss that wasn't as sweet or innocent as the earlier one.

She wrapped herself in the moment, refusing to think about the future or any implications related to kissing Clint Walker.

"A spot of tea would be delightful," he said when he finally released her, putting on a posh accent. "And if a cup of tea is a euphemism for something else, then I—"

Still in his arms, Maria tickled him without mercy. "You are such a brat. I swear it's the ocean air."

"It's not," he said, helpless with laughter.

"You are so unbelievably ticklish!"

He was handsome when he laughed, and all trace of worry left his face, giving him that youthful look that had intrigued her two days ago on the beach. It was hard to believe he'd had any sort of recent health issue.

The idea sobered her, and she relented, steering him toward the kitchen as she asked, "Fiona said you had a health scare? Everything's okay?"

She tried to keep it casual, but knew her concern had revealed itself in her voice. Worry had returned to the lines in his face.

"I'm fine."

"Are you? Because I don't want to get involved with a man who's on death's door."

"We're getting involved?" There was a warmth to his voice she wanted to keep there.

"No. But that still doesn't mean I want to be an item on someone's bucket list." With a slight amount of alarm, she realized she wanted to be a lot more than that.

"Bucket list?" he repeated.

"You know, a kiss or a girlfriend before you kick the bucket or something like that?"

"Shoot. You're onto me. The doctor found something odd with my prostate. But the delightful news is that it turned out to be nothing a dose of radiation can't fix."

Maria gasped, her palms landing lightly on his chest.

"I'm kidding." He gently took her hands, holding them in front of him, then placed a kiss on her forehead. "It was nothing more than a bit of inflammation. He fixed me up."

"I'm glad."

"Were you worried about me?" A slow smile of pleasure stretched his mouth.

"Yes." She pulled her hands from his and busied herself with gathering cups for tea.

"Less interested now that I might stick around another twenty years?" He craned his neck, trying to see her expression, and she glowered even though she didn't feel the least bit angry. "Were you afraid your new boyfriend was about to keel over?"

She sighed at his teasing.

"Maybe you thought he was looking to entrap someone to be his in-home nurse during his final days?"

She gave his shoulder a light tap of disapproval as she reached around him for the electric kettle. "Don't make me take you by your ear."

"I've heard about that infamous abuse. You have rumors being spread by your boys all over town, and yet I have never seen you get physical with a single soul. Not even that time Ryan had a fit in the middle of Main Street when he was—how old? five? seven?—because you wouldn't buy him an ice-cream cone."

Maria laughed. "Oh, that one was such a handful. If I hadn't been so tired from raising all those boys, I might've had the grace to be embarrassed."

"You handle all of life's bumps with endless grace."

"I wish that were true. I've had my share of fits over the years." Not so many, but enough that she didn't want to think about them.

Maria filled the kettle and plugged it in. She opened the cupboard above the counter. "What kind of tea do you like?"

"How about something without caffeine," Clint said, checking the clock on the oven's console.

"We haven't had lunch," Maria said with surprise. She was so out of sync with her routine, she'd missed the meal. She went to the fridge. "I could do with a sandwich. How about you?"

"Sure."

Maria moved around a few take-out containers, opening them to check the contents. "I forgot about these. Kit and I ate at Sweet Caroline's the other night and she never eats her leftovers. How about I have hers and you have mine?" She lifted her eyebrows to see if it was okay with Clint.

He peeked inside the take-out box, seeing her untouched half of chicken potpie. He picked it up and cradled it in his hand, taking a bite as he moved to the small dining nook just beyond the kitchen.

"I'll take that as a yes," she said. Men were so easy to please. They didn't need a napkin, plate or even a utensil. Just hand them the food and they were good.

With a shrug, Maria followed Clint with her own box. He hadn't stopped in the nook, but had opened the patio door and was eating at the railing that overlooked the condo's inner courtyard and pool. She took a chair behind him and he turned, settling in the one beside her, the idea of tea forgotten.

The weather was gorgeous, with a streak of sunshine warming the patio. Below, a breeze rippled the blue water of the quiet pool, where a floating leaf turned idly like a rowboat with only one oar.

When they finished eating Maria popped up, "Oh! I forgot about the tea."

The kettle had clicked off, but the water was still warm.

"The cups in here?" Clint had followed her and started opening cupboard doors at random.

"They're already on the counter." She held up two boxes of decaffeinated tea.

"Raspberry," he said.

Maria checked them. "There's no raspberry."

"Strawberry?"

"Look at the boxes already," she said with a laugh, knowing full well he could read.

With a grin, Clint tapped the blue one. "Blueberry. I don't think I've ever had it before."

"I don't think I have, either."

"It'll be our first time… together." He opened his eyes as if it was an enormous deal and she laughed as he poured water for their tea.

"Who was your first?" she asked, without thinking. His spine straightened suddenly, and he sloshed some water onto the counter. Maria waited, curious if he would answer.

"You know Daisy-Mae Ray?" he asked.

"Give me a break." Maria snorted as she grabbed a dish-cloth to sop up the spilled water. Daisy-Mae was her son Myles's age.

"Her grandma."

Maria groaned. "How is it you can always make me feel so old?"

Clint caressed her cheek. "All while making you feel so young."

"How do you do that?"

"Magic."

She leaned in, hoping for a kiss. She was rewarded.

A FEW HOURS LATER, SETTLED ON THE DECK WITH CLINT once again, the cribbage board resting on the small slated table between their deck chairs declared the truth. Maria was about to get skunked by Clint. She needed twenty-one more points to get over the skunk line, whereas he needed only ten to win.

"Who was *your* first?" he asked, after counting his hand and scoring his points. Four more to take the game.

"Roy."

Clint glanced up at her, judging her seriousness.

"I dated a few others, but Roy was my high school sweetheart."

"You married after graduation, right?"

"We waited a year and a half." It was normal in those days to marry young, rarer now. Her sons were all either nearing their thirties or already there. They were just starting to get serious about finding someone to settle down with.

"So you like older women?" Maria asked casually, thinking about Daisy-Mae Ray's grandmother.

"She's only two years older than I am. Daisy-Mae's a rarity in her family, seeing as she didn't have kids lickety-split like her mom and grandma."

"I suppose she is," Maria agreed, dealing them their next hand. "I thought for a while she and Myles might end up together."

"I was thinking it might be Jackie."

Maria nodded. She'd considered that idea fairly seriously, as well.

"Did you ever regret marrying so young?" Clint asked.

"Not really. Do you? How old were you and Kay-Lynn when you got married?"

"In our early twenties. I can't remember exactly. It was after college."

"Is that where you met?"

He nodded.

"What made you leave her?"

He looked up from his hand, his upper lip tucked under his bottom teeth as he contemplated her for a long moment. A bird fluttered by, angling as though it planned to land on the patio until it saw them and veered away. "What makes you think it was me?"

"It wasn't?"

He shook his head.

"Were you surprised?" she asked, curious about what they might have in common.

"In retrospect, no. In the moment, yes."

"That was like me and Roy," she said, starting the next round by putting down a card. "It surprised me when he voiced those thoughts. He'd gotten a lot further than I had with that line of thinking. It was unsettling how he'd allowed himself to complete that what-if. Then to keep following it until it became an actual plan." She felt the hurt, the sting, the betrayal. She'd always shut down those types of thoughts, believing the two of them would be in it together, through thick and thin, right until the end.

"Did you dispute the divorce?"

She shook her head. "If someone's that far gone, what's the point? I wasn't getting him back." They finished the hand, and Clint scored the points for them both.

"That's game."

She swept up the cards, putting them back in their box and feeling like a rebel for not shuffling them first. "Nice job on the win."

"Is there a prize?" Clint asked. His smile made her leave her old hurts behind and return to the moment. To Clint. To laughter and joy.

"There's a kiss, but only if you promise to be a good sport about winning."

"I'm always a good sport."

Maria scooted forward in her chair, leaning across the small table to give Clint a kiss that had the promise of becoming more.

She heard through the patio doors the rattle of the front door closing, then Kit calling, "I'm home!"

"We're out here," she answered, disappointed in the timing.

"I have good news," her friend announced, sliding open the patio door. "The fundraiser needs more help." There was a groan in her voice despite her cheeriness. Maria had never seen Kittim in a truly bad mood, and couldn't imagine what it might be like. She had a suspicion it might feel as though the earth had fallen off its axis.

"Oh, hi. You must be Clint," her friend said.

He stood and shook her hand.

"What are you two up to?" Kit asked as Clint offered her his chair. She declined and he sat again.

"Making out," Clint said, as Maria replied, "Playing a game of Getting My Butt Kicked at Cribbage."

Kit smiled and winked at her. "Way to go, girl." She moved back inside, calling through the open door, "I'm hungry. Do you two have plans for supper?"

Maria frowned and checked her watch. It felt like she and Clint had just eaten lunch, but it had already been hours. She checked the sky, and sure enough, the sun was dipping toward the horizon.

"Sorry, we ate your leftovers," Clint said.

"Good. I never do."

Maria watched him, curious if he thought they might have supper plans.

"I was thinking a stir-fry." Kit leaned out the glass door to address Clint. "Do you want to stay?"

"Sure." He stood up. "What can I do to help?"

"You can open the bottle of white wine I have chilling in the fridge. I'm going to change out of these clothes. Maria, can you yank the appropriate veggies out of the crisper?" Without waiting for an answer, Kit headed down the hallway toward her bedroom.

"You two have been friends a long time?" Clint asked.

Maria nodded.

"I can see why."

"How's that?" she asked as they moved to the kitchen.

"You're both good at taking charge as well as taking orders. You're a lot alike."

Maria chuckled. "I suppose that's true." Except Kit didn't seem to be having a late midlife crisis.

"She's a good friend?"

"The best." And she had been for years—ever since they'd met here one summer and she'd borrowed Kit's sunscreen on the beach. They didn't see each other often, but they kept in touch.

Clint opened the fridge, handing Maria the bottle of wine before rummaging through the other contents. He began passing her various items.

"I can do that if you want to open the wine."

"Don't trust a bachelor when it comes to vegetables?"

"Not especially. Have you met my boys? They practically died of scurvy when I left them alone on the ranch for a few months."

"It was just a ploy to get you to come home again."

Home. What was she going to do when she returned home? How was she going to resolve this feeling of being unsettled inside? And what was she going to do about Clint?

She placed a hand against his back as he continued his search through the fridge, and said, "I don't know how this can work once we return to Sweetheart Creek."

"How's that?"

"The boys. The ranch. Life."

"Well..." Clint straightened, his brow furrowed in thought. "I'll have to convince them you absolutely need me in your life."

"How will you do that?" she asked, curious if he was serious or not.

"I'll explain how it'll be a horrible future for all of us without me around. There'll be no lasagna or cinnamon buns, because you'll be too bereft to cook. It's to everyone's advantage to have me with you." He closed the fridge and began opening the bottle of wine, his eyes never leaving hers.

"I see."

He poured three glasses while she thought over the logistics of them continuing a relationship back home.

Clint handed her a glass, then lifted his own. "Cheers to that?"

She sighed and clinked her glass against his. "Cheers."

She gestured to the stack of vegetables he'd pulled from the fridge. "Are you going to surprise me with those deft skills of yours, master chef? Or do I have to cook?"

"I will always do more than merely surprise you, Maria. You can count on that."

CHAPTER 6

Clint had taken over the kitchen, creating a marvelous stir-fry. Afterward, Kit had fallen asleep on the couch and he'd tipped his head toward the door with a finger to his lips, pulling Maria by the hand.

They'd slipped out and were now walking hand in hand past beach houses, admiring the wreaths, lights and other Christmas decorations.

"Thanks for supper," she said, swinging his hand in hers.

"You know, I'm okay just dating. We don't need to get married."

She laughed, peering up into the dark sky. "We don't?"

"I'm serious." He stopped walking. "I know your boys and your family are important to you. So is the ranch."

She swallowed the apprehension swelling inside her. She wanted to talk about this, but was afraid where it might lead, and that she might wind up without Clint.

"Your family needs things from you, and you want to provide whatever it is. There's nothing wrong with that. You're integral." He spoke faster so she wouldn't interrupt. "But what about you, Maria?" Her name rolled off his tongue

81

in that sweet way she loved. "Ignoring everything that pricks at your sense of obligation, what do *you* want? Really and truly?"

"Really and truly?"

"Yes."

"For us?" she asked, wanting to unleash all her hopes and dreams, but afraid if she opened her mouth they would all spill out.

"One wish." They had stopped walking near a yard that was glowing with lights. "But not about you and me. Blurt it out."

"I want Cole to come home." The pain was clear to her own ears. "For Christmas, if not forever. He's been gone too long. I miss him and it's not right that he's been away forever."

Clint was quiet for a moment and she was left with nothing but her own thoughts and emotions, wondering what kind of woman he might consider her to be. What mother allowed her son to run off and stay away for almost five years?

Maybe she wasn't the woman Clint thought she was.

She knew she'd done things she'd never expected. Life unfolded. Events happened. And sometimes afterward you picked yourself up out of the dirt, pulling emotional shrapnel from your soul and wondering what the heck had just occurred.

But when it came right down to it, a good mother didn't allow her son to have that much space.

"Well?" Clint asked.

"Well what?" she snapped, immediately regretting her tone. She murmured an apology.

He ignored it and said, "How are you going to remedy this?"

"I thought we were talking about you and me?"

He lifted a shoulder casually. "We got sidetracked by other things you want and need. So what are you going to do? What's your plan?"

"I don't have one."

"You make things happen everywhere you go, and you're a woman of action." His tone was persuasive. "I bet you at least have an idea."

Maria mulled that over, her spirits lifting.

Clint gently nudged her. He was watching her with questioning eyes. "You think maybe you could call him?"

She was already shaking her head. "I don't think I can."

"Why not?"

"Words were exchanged, and I'm not sure he wants to talk to me."

What must her son think of her for not reaching out? For not trying? For letting Roy speak for both of them.

"Call him," Clint said, placing a hand over hers.

"I'm ashamed to admit that I don't have his current number."

"Do you know who does?"

"Brant." For too long, she had left her middle son, the sensitive one, with that burden. Where had she been in her life? Had she really been that absent for so long?

It hurt to think, breathe, exist.

She'd sided with Roy during a pivotal fight between him and Cole, because that's what she'd thought she was supposed to do. She hadn't gone after her son afterward, even though she'd known he'd been in such pain.

When the boys were small and had started to find cracks and loopholes in their parenting front, as kids do, she and Roy had vowed to remain united. They'd been outnumbered, and knew they had to stand back-to-back if they wanted to retain control over their sons.

They'd been good at staying united. Too good, maybe.

The habit had been ingrained, but now Roy had moved on. Did that mean she could, as well? Did they no longer have to stand together when it came to their sons? Could she speak her mind? Reach out to Cole and mend things? She'd always thought Roy was wrong, and now their actions and identities were distinct from each other. But she couldn't betray or undermine him like that. He was still Cole's father.

"Would Brant give you the number?" Clint asked.

"I don't know," she whispered.

It was wrong to remain silent and allow Cole to be alone for another Christmas.

Clint cupped her cheek. She nuzzled in ever so slightly and his thumb brushed her skin, causing her to shiver.

"What would you say to him if you could phone him?"

She was certain she wouldn't be able to speak. That familiar voice would bring instant tears to her eyes. But she knew what she'd say.

"I'd ask him to come home."

She winced against the pain. It was selfish to want him to return. If he did, it would upset April's life, and she was just getting settled again. And it would interfere with Brant's life just when he was finally being noticed by the woman he'd loved for years.

Nobody else likely noticed that, but Maria had. She was a mom. She had to look out for her entire flock. But to keep sacrificing Cole felt wrong. It was time for everyone to stand on their own two feet.

And maybe that was what she was here to do. Learn how to let them do that.

"What else?" Clint asked. He'd pulled out his phone and was typing something.

"A Christmas visit would be nice," she said, tipping her chin up. She angled closer to his screen. Did he have Cole's number?

Because she wasn't going to call him. Not yet. Even though she wanted her boy to know he was always welcome and always wanted.

Clint lowered his phone, putting it into his back pocket and making her relax.

"I hope he's a good man," she said, watching him. "I hope he's treating others right."

He pulled his phone from his pocket again and gazed at it, then turned it toward her. A text message lit up the screen, featuring a phone number. "Why don't you call him and find out?"

She inhaled, her fingers going to her lips. Cole's number. He had Cole's number.

He'd gotten it. For her.

Clint slowly offered her the phone. She shook her head and backed up a step.

"I can't. I miss him, but this is about more than me. More than him." She was still shaking her head. "I have to think about this. I can't just call."

MARIA HUNCHED OVER A CANVAS BAG, STITCHING A CANDY cane wound with red string onto the handle. She'd hoped taking on this task for the fundraiser would keep her mind off Clint and last night's conversation about Cole. So far it hadn't.

Pressing her left hand to her lower back, she arched her spine and studied her completed work spread out on the dining nook's table. All morning she'd ignored texts from Clint, as well as from the ranch. Kit had gone in to work and Maria had taken the time and space to think.

So far she hadn't come to any conclusions. Not about

Cole. Not about Clint. Not even about what she wanted the next segment of her life to look like.

The door to the condo opened, and Maria checked the time. Kit's lunch break.

"Those look good," Clint said, entering the room and seeming to take all the air with him. Maria fought the urge to cross the space and slip into his arms for a much-needed hug.

Too many thoughts. Too many emotions. And right now he looked like he always did—a rock to cling to as she weathered the storm.

"You got a lot done," Kit said, coming in behind Clint and scanning the table. "Did you see who I found on my walk home?" She moved past Clint and into the kitchen.

He leaned against the wall, watching Maria. "Need help?"

She shook her head and threaded the needle for another bag.

"We got the first coat of blue on the scooter. You were right. It looks good. Very cute."

"You know what would make those bags look even better?" Kit called from the kitchen.

"What?" Maria called back.

"A hand-painted scene."

"You could paint them," Clint said, coming closer. "Like a scene from your ornament."

"That was uninspired and boring."

"It was special, a scene from the beach here in town. People would love it."

Kittim entered the room again. "I agree. It would be a hit."

Maria laughed. "You realize he's trying to convince me to paint something on all the bags." She gestured toward the tall stack. The Morrison Mansion's ballroom would be stuffed with guests on Saturday night. She couldn't paint something for everyone.

"But it's a cute idea," Kit said.

"I thought so," Clint agreed.

"It would be a tremendous amount of work."

"What if it was just for the sponsors?" Kit's eyes lit up and she clapped her hands together. "They'd love that! A hand-painted scene on their bags to show them how special they are to us."

"How many sponsors are there?" Clint asked.

"Not that many."

"Five? Fifty?" Maria asked.

"Would you do ten? That would cover our gold level sponsors."

Maria eyed the bags. Ten would be okay. If she could find a shred of creativity within her. "I'll think about it."

"That's a no." Kit pouted.

"Maybe not," Clint said, going to stand behind Maria. He started to massage her shoulders, like he'd promised to do if she painted the scooter for him. Instinctively she tightened her muscles, nervous about what accepting the back rub might mean.

Men left when they got bored, and she wasn't much more than who she was in this moment.

"Relax," he coaxed.

"I'm trying."

"It's just a massage," he said.

"I know."

"I'm going to zip over to the neighbor's," Kit said, watching them with a smile. "She has something for the silent auction. Back in a flash. Be good!"

"Take your time," Clint called back.

Kit giggled as the door closed.

Clint leaned forward, his breath tickling Maria's ear as he whispered, "It's not a marriage proposal." He bent farther to catch her eye, then gave her a devilish wink. "Yet."

She laughed, waving him away. After yesterday's joke to Miss Lucille, saying they weren't married yet, and now this, she was having shivers of anticipation over when he might ask her on an official date.

A date.

How had he got her to a place where she was longing for that?

"There really is something about the ocean air that makes you misbehave like a young boy."

"Maybe it's the company." His hands returned to her shoulders.

"I don't seem to turn you into a brat back in Sweetheart Creek."

"Back home you're always racing off somewhere, saving lives and putting out fires."

She pursed her lips. "I am not."

His powerful hands found the exact knot she couldn't seem to work out on her own. She relented, relaxing into his fingers. "And yet here you are again."

"What does that mean?"

"You're taking care of others instead of yourself. Even with this—" he gestured to the canvas bags "—you're taking care of others."

She failed to see a problem with that.

"This is your vacation, is it not?"

"And?"

"And you're helping people."

He was still working the knot in her shoulder, and she moaned as the muscle loosened. It was as if years of tension were melting from her back.

Clint went to work on the left shoulder, and she rolled her neck to the other side, giving him more room for his large hands to manipulate the tightness.

"That's from carrying everyone," he said, his voice deep and rich in Maria's ear.

"But who would I be if I wasn't helping?" she asked, not expecting an answer. "That's who I was raised to be. That's who I am. People leave holes and I fill them."

"You do." His voice was tender, with no hint of judgment, and his acknowledgment brought a wash of emotion.

"What's wrong with that?"

"Nothing. Nothing at all. But why not combine the two?"

"The two what?"

"You doing things for you, and this volunteer work. Do them together."

"You lost me."

"Paint, Maria." He sat in the chair beside her.

"I'm not—"

He shushed her. "It doesn't have to be a new career or for a bigger purpose. It can be for fun. I saw you with that ornament in Coastal Creations. The total concentration, the small smile playing at your lips. You enjoyed it. Time flew, didn't it?"

"Yeah, but—"

"No buts. We'll pick up what you need so you can release your inner artist. It'll be a two-for-one deal."

She leaned back in her chair and crossed her arms. "And if I say no?"

"Then I'll paint them."

She laughed, thinking what joyful fun creations he might make. "I think I'd like that."

"Maria, that was a threat."

She laughed even harder.

Clint slid his hands across her shoulders, turning her so her back was to him again. His arms went across her collarbone as he pulled her against his chest. He was hugging her, she realized, relishing his warmth against her right shoulder and part of her spine, his arms holding her close as his cheek nestled in the crook of her neck.

It was an odd feeling, and it reminded her of when the boys were adolescents. They'd ambush her with a quick hug from behind, needing the contact, but not the full-on mother hug that would embarrass them.

And yet this was different. She could lean on Clint, let it all go.

"Who would I be if I didn't do these things?" she asked, curious to hear his answer.

"You would be you."

"But who is that?"

His arms tightened around her. "You didn't believe me when I told you who I see?" Clint's embrace loosened like a knot under water, flowing away as he shifted to see her better. "Or were you just not listening?" His tone was teasing, but he reached across her face, stroking a thumb over her right cheek, and she shivered. The gesture was a test. A move that could be brushed off or taken as something more intimate.

She waited to see if he would do it again, what his next move would be.

"You weren't listening, were you?" he scolded. "Or maybe you just love hearing good things said about yourself."

"Maybe."

"You're an amazing woman, Maria, and I'd be honored to be your date."

"You would?" she asked, amusement lacing her voice. When was the last time a man had been honored to go some-where with her? "Wait, are you avoiding my question?"

"Yes, because I hate to repeat myself. You need to relax and enjoy yourself." His tone was serious but playful, and she wasn't sure how to take him. "Unfortunately, though, I can't be your date for the gala."

"We'll both be home before then."

Silence stretched between them. No doubt he was thinking the same thing—what would happen when they returned home? Would they ignore each other? Try to sort out how to pursue this friendship?

Friendship. It already felt like more than that.

"Instead we'll have to have our own date tomorrow night before my flight. I'll borrow Jeff's truck and pick you up at five."

"Wait." Maria shut her eyes, backtracking through the conversation. "A date?" She leaned forward and turned as he released her, studying his expression. She couldn't read his tone, but knew his eyes would give him away. Or at least hoped they would.

He had a bemused expression, the kindness in his eyes letting her know she could be herself with him, question things, make demands, and never affront him. But was he serious about a date? He knew this thing they were doing would turn into a mess once they were home.

Wouldn't it?

"Go with it, Maria," he said, his eyes dancing. "If I have to trick you into going out with me, then let it be. I already said yes."

She chuckled, delighted by his ploy. He smiled back, the skin around his dark eyes crinkling. It was difficult to be too serious for too long while near him. He brought life and joy with him everywhere he went.

She knew he was being extra charming to woo her, but she'd also known him for years and knew this was a big part of who he was. Naturally. Even when she wasn't around.

She caught herself leaning closer, waiting, wondering, dreaming. Clint would make a fine boyfriend. She already knew that. She enjoyed spending time with him; he made her laugh, was sweet and thoughtful, and felt like someone she could pour her heart out to.

She caught herself and straightened. "You know that anything that happens here won't make it back to Sweetheart Creek. My boys…" She paused, thinking how they might react if she came home with a boyfriend. And how would it work, bringing him to the ranch that had always belonged to Wylders?

"Your sons are adults," Clint said. "And so are you. And so am I."

"And I don't think I could bear inviting drama into my life right now."

"Then let's not make it dramatic."

She felt a stir of discontentment inside. "We're too old. Our time has passed." She stood, feeling a great tearing in her heart. "I'm sorry. I can't pretend I'm ready for something like this."

"How about I simply escort you to dinner tomorrow?"

"Clint…"

"I'm serious."

"So am I. What happens between us in Indigo Bay—"

"Will be magnificent, spectacular, and something we will never forget." Clint had stood up as well. He reached for her hand and held it lightly. "Know that if I fall in love with you here, I'm taking that home with me. Life is short, Maria. So here's the truth." He studied their hands for a beat before looking up, determination in his steady gaze. "I'm fighting for you whether you're ready or not."

MARIA, STILL DAZED FROM CLINT'S PROCLAMATION, CHUCKED tubes of paint at random into her basket.

"Are you sure you need this much pink?" Kittim asked, holding up a handful of reddish hues.

"What?"

"What did Clint say to you before we left? You're on a different planet, and it seems like it might be a hostile one."

Maria blinked away her thoughts and focused on her friend, the craft store and her basket. Kit had returned from the neighbor's moments after Clint had proclaimed he wasn't giving up on Maria and a romance. She'd said the first thing she could think of to Kit.

Paint.

She needed paint for the bags. Immediately. Before her ideas dried up.

Her friend had squealed in excitement and swept her off like Maria had hoped she would.

The problem was, Maria didn't particularly want to create something for each bag, but she'd needed space. How could Clint be so sure? How could he be ready to fight for her? It had to be lingering feelings from his health scare. He was primed to leap on anything that moved and hang on tight in fear of losing it.

Maria's phone buzzed in her pocket.

"Is that Levi again?" Kit asked.

She pulled out the cell and glanced at the screen. He'd already called her once and she'd ignored it. She nodded and went back to selecting paint, only this time with more care and attention.

"You know I don't mind if you pick up. I mean, if there's an emergency…" Kit was watching her from the corner of her eyes.

"There isn't."

The phone continued to buzz in Maria's pocket.

"Did the boys say something?"

"I'm trying to have a vacation."

Feeling Kit's eyes on her, she explained, "They keep asking me about every little thing like they're afraid to make a decision without me, but I know they know how to run the place. I don't know where I fit into their worlds any longer, but this constant asking me about all these small things isn't working. And then Clint had the gall to say he wants me and will fight for me. How is that going to work? He wants to date. Like, seriously date." She threw up her hands, rattling everything in the basket slung over her arm.

She was trying to relax, but still had one foot back on the ranch, still needed that sense of control over everything. Why couldn't she step away for a few days?

"You need to take a breath, woman," Kittim said with a light laugh. "You need some time for yourself or something."

"I'm trying! That's why I'm here."

Kittim gnawed on her bottom lip, her eyes wide.

"I'm sorry." Maria sighed and added a few brushes to her basket, but they slid out the holes and onto the floor.

"Hey, no need to apologize." Kit folded her in a quick hug before she could stoop down to collect them. "I get it."

"I feel like I need boundaries between me and the ranch when I'm away. I want to be important to them, but I also want some peace. I've already learned that I need the ranch in my life, but this all feels so difficult."

Her phone buzzed yet again. Kit reached over and fished it out of Maria's pocket, then tapped the screen a few times and put it to her ear. Moments later she said, "Levi, honey, it's Kittim. You need to let your mother enjoy her vacation, okay?" She listened. "It's a tractor. Fix it or buy a new one." She listened for another moment. "I know, but you're a big boy. You can settle this. Your mom left you in charge of the ranch for a reason. Figure it out and let her enjoy her last two days, okay?" She rolled her eyes as she listened some more. "I have a feeling you already know what she wants done with the machine."

Maria nodded.

"So quit dragging your feet and make it happen. Or at the very least deal with it all when she gets home." She tapped the end call button with a flourish and handed back the phone.

"How did that go?"

"You know... Whine, whine, whine." She winked. "It's fine. He's just trying to do the right thing."

They moved toward the checkout. "So, solved that one. Want to talk about your identity issues next, or should we jump right into your love life?"

"Neither of those are as easy as telling Levi to lay off for a few days."

They laughed and Maria pulled Kit into a one-armed hug. "Thanks."

"Anytime." She studied her as they faced each other in the lineup. "So? What are you going to do about Clint?"

"I have absolutely no clue."

"Make a wish and hope it comes true?"

Maria's thoughts floated toward the Christmas tree set up in downtown Indigo Bay. Maybe she should have made a second wish the other day.

"He stayed on here a few extra days, you know," Maria said, without thought.

"For you?"

She nodded. They'd reached the front of the line, and she unloaded her basket for the checkout clerk.

"And?"

"He wants to pursue things. Seriously. Even back home."

"And?"

"And it won't work, obviously." Surely her friend understood all the reasons that idea was a nonstarter.

"You think the boys would be upset?"

She nodded.

"They're adults, Maria." Kit rolled her eyes and swiped her credit card to pay for the items. "They need to get over themselves."

Maria held in a painful breath.

They had gotten over Roy and Sophia, but how often did they get together with their dad? Not regularly. Roy might be okay with that, but Maria wanted to see her boys as often as possible, even though they were all grown up.

And if her actions upset them while they were all living on the same ranch, how would that go? Not well. And not worth it.

"Do you need me to call Levi?" Kit began fishing in Maria's pocket and she laughed and stepped out of reach.

"I'll do it, you know," Kit threatened, taking the shopping bag. "You deserve love. Anyway, they're probably just not used to the idea of you with someone else. Or, for that matter, their mom wanting and needing love." They headed out the door into the afternoon warmth, where the smell of ocean salt filled the air. "How did they react to Roy and Sophia?"

Maria shrugged. "Okay."

"Are you too afraid to demand the same level of respect from them?"

"It's different."

"Bull crap. That thinking keeps women in their place." They moved across the parking lot to Kit's car. "Go find Clint. Kiss him. See what happens. Let the future in. And you know what I always say about the future."

"What?"

"It's in the future. Don't worry about it."

Maria just shook her head.

"I'm serious. Quit being a chicken and go." Kit gave her a push as though she had a destination in mind.

"Go to Clint?"

"Yes."

"And do what?"

"What I just told you to do." Kit unlocked her driver's-side door, then opened it with an exasperated flourish.

"Now?"

"Now."

"I don't know."

Kit tossed the bag of supplies onto the passenger seat. "Since when has Maria Wylder been afraid of anything? Those boys can handle more than you realize. Quit babying them and go get your life back. Starting with that man who makes you light up every time you think of him."

She got into the car and let down the passenger-side window. Maria tried the door. Still locked.

"I'm sorry, but you need some tough love right now, sweetie." Kit gave her a forgive-me smile and put the car in gear. "You can thank me later!"

Maria, too stunned to do anything, watched as her friend drove away.

CHAPTER 7

"*K*it says I need to get my life back."

There was a moment of silence on the other end, and Maria wondered if her cell phone had lost its connection to Clint's. She supposed, though, there wasn't much of a reply to that statement. It also wasn't much of a conversation opener when you were calling someone you'd just fled from.

Did she really light up every time she thought about Clint, as Kit had said? She checked her reflection in the craft store window. She was smiling.

He'd made a grand proclamation she couldn't handle. One that had been completely over the top for this stage of their relationship, and her best friend had just driven off and left her in the middle of town.

And she was smiling.

She needed to get her head checked.

Finally, Clint made a sound on the other end of the line, letting her know he'd heard her statement about needing to reclaim the interests in her life.

"She left me outside the craft store."

He made another small sound of acknowledgment.

"I'm sorry I ran out of the condo."

"You know you're important to me, right?" he said at long last. She didn't answer, and he added, "And I understand that it scares you."

It did. It scared her a lot, but she couldn't figure out why.

No, she knew. She feared he would sweep her into his world, she'd fall in love, wrap her life around his, and then he'd leave. One day… he'd just go. Like her dad had. Like Roy had.

There had been signs, of course, but with her father she'd been too young to understand what they'd meant. With Roy she hadn't believed he'd truly leave after all they'd been through together.

"I want to date you even when we go home, and our real lives intrude and everyone gets nosy and interferes," Clint said. His voice was gentle, but firm. He knew what he wanted with such certainty. But how long would it last? How long before it changed into something resembling apathy?

She made a small sound.

"Did Kit really leave you at the craft store?"

"She was instituting tough love, apparently."

He chuckled.

"She told me to reclaim my life." She sighed, shaking her head at the moving clouds above.

"Sounds like that could get epic. Where are you?"

"Downtown. I can walk back to the condo." It would probably take her half an hour, but she'd walked farther and in worse weather.

"I know a guy with a scooter. He could swing by and pick you up."

She hesitated. She wasn't sure if he meant himself or not.

"It's me, Maria," he said, laughter in his voice, as though he was sensing her doubts. "I'm the guy with a scooter."

"I knew that."

"Be there in five?" The question in his voice warmed her.

Was that why she'd called him? For a rescue? Or had it to do with that something that made her smile when she thought of him? That something she couldn't seem to escape, even when she tried to run from it.

"That would be nice," she said.

She ended the call, wishing they had more time in Indigo Bay to sort things out. They had only a day and a half left, and that wasn't long.

What would they do? Could they bring this home to Sweetheart Creek like he believed? Before she could sort out her thoughts, the scooter glided up in front of the craft store, Clint looking like a hero on his robin's egg colored machine.

"It's blue!" she said, grinning. It looked good. Fresh, bright and retro. The thing had adventure and fun stamped all over it.

"One more coat of blue to go, then a clear one and it's done."

"But you'll dirty it driving around town. You're going to have to clean it again."

He gave a small nod.

"I could have walked."

"When are you going to learn you're important to me?" he asked, handing her a helmet. "Everything that's important to you is important to me."

"Everything?" she joked, reaching for it. He didn't let go until she looked up, met his eyes.

"Every little thing," he said with emphasis, warming her from the toes upward.

He slipped off the machine as she put on the headgear, then helped her onto the small seat behind the driver's. When they were both aboard he looked over his shoulder. "Do you want to drive?"

She shook her head. She was fine with him taking the lead on the small machine.

As they drove down the streets of Indigo Bay, they passed a stately woman walking her small fluffy dog. Miss Lucille.

"Told you it would look cute!" Clint called to her. She flinched when he merrily tooted the horn.

Maria giggled and wrapped her arms tighter around his waist even though she didn't need to. His body relaxed, melting into her a little more.

"I'm supposed to be painting those stupid bags, but let's go play hooky for a little while," she called to him when he switched lanes to turn toward the condo.

He sped up, moving back into his original lane, then turning onto a narrow road that would take them along the beach. Maria smiled, feeling as though she was living someone else's life. The thrumming of her pulse, the ocean air, riding on a scooter with a man who wanted to win her heart…

Maybe he already had.

Maybe things were already perfect, and she just had her head stuck in the logistics. Maybe she needed to listen to Kit and allow the future to be where it was supposed to—in the future.

Look at her son Levi, and his girlfriend. Laura was from New York City, and a fashion model by trade. Levi was from out in the boonies, his life devoted to the family ranch. Yet somehow the two of them were making it work, logistics be damned.

And Maria had raised him. Surely she could make something work between herself and a man who lived just a few miles away.

"Okay," she said over the wind.

Clint pointed toward a small pullout ahead on the sandy shore. "Here?"

"No. *Okay*." She put special emphasis on the word, knowing he'd understand.

He let up on the throttle as the meaning sank in. "Okay?"

She tightened her arms around him. She wasn't ready to say he was her boyfriend, and it felt odd to say they were dating. But that's what she wanted. When she went home, she wanted more moments and afternoons just like this one, even though there'd be no ocean, no salty air, no scooter. But there would be the most important thing—Clint. He made each day interesting and special. And they could have moments like this anywhere, if they tried. Even in Sweetheart Creek.

"Let's date. Slow and steady, though," she warned, hoping to temper his enthusiasm before he ran away with his expectations.

"Slow and steady? What does that look like?"

"We'll figure it out later. Let's enjoy playing hooky, and then you can take me out for supper, instead of tomorrow night."

"You know the best part of playing hooky is making out somewhere, right?"

She laughed, her entire body feeling lighter and freer than it had in years. There was something very special about her sweet joymaker, Clint Walker.

"Hello?" Maria said, after picking up her phone. She was almost ready to go out for supper with Clint. Okay, it was a date. She wouldn't kid herself any longer, and was unable to disguise the happiness in her voice even though caller ID informed her it was her ex-husband on the other end of the line.

"Maria?" he asked, as though unable to identify her,

despite having shared forty years of marriage. The past year apart sure must have been a kicker if he had trouble recognizing her voice. Or maybe he just didn't expect her to sound happy.

That was a sobering thought.

"Yes, Roy?" she said with exaggerated patience, a tone he was well familiar with, suggesting she wasn't in the mood for dickering.

"You just sounded different," he said defensively. "I'm calling about Christmas."

Christmas… Should she get Clint a gift? Maybe it was too soon. Definitely too soon to spend the holiday together.

"It's on the twenty-fifth," she said, biting the inside of her cheek to prevent herself from laughing at her own attitude. "It's on a Friday this year."

"I know when it is." She could tell by his sharpness that her joyful mood had put him off his own.

No doubt the man knew she was in Indigo Bay at the moment, and was probably wondering what she was up to, and whether she was visiting his family and spreading lies. Because, sadly, that was what her ex-husband had become: suspicious. Their divorce, though taking her by surprise, had been mutual, and she had no plans to taint the waters with his family after so many years of having his back.

"Well then?" she asked kindly. "Are you wondering what you should get me?"

"I'm calling to ask what you're going to do about Christmas," Roy scolded. "What are we going to do about the boys?"

"I'll buy them gifts from myself and I'm sure you will do the same."

"I meant Christmas Day. Where will you be?"

"I will be at the ranch, just like I am every year." She'd missed spending only one Christmas morning there—last year. She'd moved into town just before the holidays, and

Christmas morning alone in town had nearly done her in, waiting for it to be time to join her family on the ranch for supper.

When Roy had moved off the ranch in June to marry Sophia, Maria's first instinct had been to move back. However, she'd refrained until autumn, knowing by then that Sweet Meadows Ranch was truly what she wanted and where she was meant to be.

"You can't kick me out of my home on Christmas Day," Roy protested.

"You left by your own volition. You are now living in a new home, with your new wife. I am on the ranch, right where I'm supposed to be. We are all happy."

"I shouldn't feel like a guest on the ranch I was raised on," he grumbled. "I can't believe I have to ask for permission to come to my own home."

"You don't have to ask for permission, and that ranch was my home for forty years. I have every right—"

"And it was mine for sixty!"

"You don't turn sixty for another three months." She said it calmly, realizing that a fight wouldn't help anything, and would likely please Roy. "I had every right to move back out there when you left. I put blood, sweat and tears and hard work into that ranch, as did you. You're no longer there, and that place needs me. Our boys need me. Carmichael is my father as much as yours."

When Roy sputtered a protest, she raised her voice to speak over him. "Do you know he has arthritis in his knees and can barely move when there's a good storm blowing in? Are you there taking care of him? Making sure he eats his vegetables and goes to the doctor? Are you stepping in to cook meals for our boys when they go down two belt sizes? Are you there showing them they can work together to run that ranch you walked away from? Or helping them through the bumps of figuring out how to love a woman? Have you not noticed our sons are growing up?" She stopped speaking, the lump in her throat too tight to speak past.

"And you're there mothering them," Roy said, his tone grumpy.

He sounded like Clint. As if mothering her boys was a terrible thing.

She supposed to them it was. They wanted that attention and energy put into them.

"And I will be there for them until the day I die."

She almost ended the call, but instead sucked in a deep breath and carried on in a civil tone. "You are always welcome to join us at Christmas, as is Sophia. You don't need an invitation. But know that I will always be there at Christmas. That is my home. That is my family. And nobody can convince me there is a better place for me to be."

Then she hit the End Call button with a flourish, but her earlier joy had vanished.

CLINT HELD THE DOOR TO KATIE'S KITCHEN, A RESTAURANT on Bayview with a Caribbean-themed decor, and ushered Maria in. Once they were settled with glasses of wine, he took her hand across the table. Maria inhaled, absorbing the ambience. Christmas songs played softly in the background, kettle drums being incorporated into the tunes to give a Caribbean feel.

Clint's phone rang, and he silenced it. "How was the rest of your day after we played hooky?"

"You can answer that if you'd like." She pointed toward his cell.

"Nobody's more important than you are right now."

"Sweet talker."

He smiled in agreement. "So? The rest of your day was good?"

Maria thought back. They'd been cramming so much into each day, maximizing their time away. They'd go off to do their own thing for an hour or two before meeting up again.

It had been only that afternoon that Kit had left her outside the craft store. And only a few hours ago that she'd decided that yes, she wanted to date Clint once they returned to Sweetheart Creek.

One more day together. What would it bring?

Maria squeezed Clint's hand, a sense of anticipation building inside her.

"Did you start painting?"

She shook her head. Not much had happened since they'd seen each other a few hours ago. She grimaced, thinking about Roy's call, and Clint shifted forward, catching her brief switch in moods. He raised his chin as an invitation to discuss what was on her mind.

"Roy called to ask about Christmas," she revealed.

"Sharing Christmas isn't easy."

"How do you and Kay-Lynn manage the holidays?" Clint had two grown kids of his own. They lived in San Antonio now and had families themselves, Kay-Lynn having moved to the city with their preteens after the divorce.

Clint leaned back in his chair, his hand sliding out of her grip. He looked uncomfortable as he ran his palms down his thighs, exhaling slowly, his eyes on a dancing Santa wearing a Rastafarian hat complete with fake dreadlocks.

"It's that bad?" Maria asked.

"No, not anymore," he said quickly, though pain was evident in his eyes. "It was when the kids were younger."

"So how did you get to where you are now—not so bad?"

He gave a wry smile that didn't reach his eyes. "The kids grew up."

"Well, mine already are, so I suppose that's a plus." It still didn't make it easy, though.

"Christmas Day doesn't mean as much as it once did."

Maria felt the muscles in her face slacken.

"No, I meant that sometimes the kids and I celebrate on the day, or before, or after. I learned that it's just as special, whenever we get together. Christmas is about time with the kids."

"I'm still at the greedy stage, where I want to spend all of Christmas with my boys."

He didn't laugh, as she expected. "I think a mom always will." His words were carefully chosen. "And I also think with you living on the ranch with several of them, it feels natural to wake up and spend Christmas morning together. Then the rest of the day."

"I told Roy that he and Sophia are welcome to join us. He feels he needs an invitation because he's become a guest in his childhood home." Maria studied the tablecloth, a blend of Christmas and beach patterns. Her heart felt heavy. She hadn't ousted Roy, and she knew it wasn't her fault he felt that way about the ranch.

"He left the place, didn't he?" Clint asked.

"Yeah, but now I live there again. I don't think he saw that one coming."

"I don't see Sophia as the ranching type."

"Oh, she's not," Maria said quickly. That was the key reason Roy had moved to town.

"Then I think this is a Roy problem, not a Maria problem."

"I know."

"But you still feel responsible, don't you?"

She nodded and took a sip of her wine.

"I have faith the two of you will work it out. And it gets easier with each passing year."

"Does it?"

"You know, after Kay-Lynn left me—"

"Why did she?"

Clint inhaled breath between his teeth, then blew it out. "You would think after all these years I would understand it a bit better."

"You don't know?"

"Apparently I was never her true love." He had reached for Maria's hand, but then withdrew his own, studying her.

"What?"

He shook his head, looking away. "Nothing."

She wondered if he feared he might be moving too fast, repeating old mistakes. Thinking she was the new Kay-Lynn. Just like she sometimes caught herself thinking he might leave her, like Roy had.

But Clint hadn't left his wife.

He had followed Maria to a different state for a vacation, in fact. Was he thinking it was love? Or was it simply an opportunity to get to know her better?

If they'd stayed in Sweetheart Creek, how long would it have taken them to reach this level of trust and affection? Years? Here, it had taken only a few days.

"I'm glad you came to Indigo Bay," she said.

"Are you?"

"I am." She smiled. Friendship, laughter, joy. That's how she'd sum up this vacation. And kisses. Lots of wonderful kisses.

"I'm glad, too."

They were silent for a moment.

"So? Tell me about these bags you needed to race out and buy paint for. They're for the gala's gold-level sponsors? Or did you just say you wanted to paint them in order to escape a man who was getting all serious on you?" He rested his arms on the table, leaning forward.

She laughed. "As embarrassing as it is, both."

"Well, I guess whatever gets you back into the groove of painting again is worth it."

"Really, I am so sorry for running out on you."

Their appetizer arrived, interrupting her apology.

"I tend to move fast," Clint said, dunking a pita chip in the shared bowl of cheese dip.

They both moaned as the rich food hit the spot. They were starting to make a dent in it when Maria's phone rang, the sound causing a few people to glance her way. She reached into her jacket pocket, hitting the silence button, then glanced at the screen, noting it was Levi. She put the phone back in her pocket.

When she glanced up, Clint was watching her. "Answer it."

She shook her head. "It's Levi. I'm sure it's not important."

Clint looked thoughtful for a moment. "You should call him back."

"Why?" He had silenced his phone, but she should answer hers? What was that about? Or was it a way to prove to her that her boys were important and it was okay if they intruded?

Or did he sense something was wrong back home? A stab of worry surged through her, and she pulled her phone out, debating.

Clint gave her a nod, and she dialed quickly. "Levi? Is everything okay?"

"Yeah. How are things?"

Maria felt her body sag. He was interrupting her date to ask how she was doing? She gave Clint a dry look and mouthed, *"Not an emergency."*

Clint frowned at her in confusion, peering at her lips. She shook her head again and waved her hand. "Did you need something, Levi?" she asked.

"Yeah, I'm trying to get ahold of Clint Walker for something. He wouldn't happen to be with you, would he?"

Maria straightened her spine. "Why?"

"Mrs. Fisher said you were going out for supper."

"Yeah, why?"

"Can you hand him the phone? I tried calling him directly already." His tone was amused.

"You did? Why?"

Levi laughed. "Mom?"

"Fine." She thrust her phone toward Clint. "He wants to talk to you."

What was going on?

Clint frowned and glanced around. He lifted the phone to his ear. "Clint here."

Maria couldn't hear Levi, only Clint's end of things. Definitely mechanical. Not what-are-you-doing-having-supper-with-my-mom.

Why would she even think that he'd call to meddle in her affairs? Because Levi always changed the subject whenever Clint came up in conversation. He clearly wasn't comfortable with the idea of her dating.

"Is everything okay?" she asked, interrupting.

Clint nodded, then looked down at the tablecloth again. "I can order the part. Yes. No, there's time. I'll order it tonight and it'll be in tomorrow or the next day." He ended the call.

"What was that about? Is he still trying to fix that old tractor? He's going to send good money after bad."

"He has a few projects on the go," Clint acknowledged. He handed back her phone. "Supper should be here soon. I'm hungry." He glanced around the bustling restaurant.

"So everything is okay?" Maria confirmed, feeling as though she was still missing a piece of the puzzle.

Clint nodded. "Just thinking through some logistics.

Christmas always throws a kink in business plans. At least it's not midweek this year."

"You know, if it's for Levi, he's fine having it done in January. There's nothing urgent on the ranch at the moment. He's my take-charge bossy son and sometimes he gets all worked up over nothing. Takes on other people's problems to solve as his own."

Clint didn't say anything, and she had a sudden, awful feeling that maybe he and her eldest son might never get along.

THEY FINISHED SUPPER, THEN CLINT GAVE MARIA A RIDE HOME in Sonja's borrowed car.

"Thanks for supper," she said, as they pulled up outside Kittim's condo.

"My pleasure."

"I'm going to paint some bags tonight. Are you going to come up and massage my shoulders?" She gave him a shy smile, feeling flirtatious and at the same time self-conscious.

"While I'd love to see your artistic side in action again, I think I'd better order some parts so they're in the shop for when I get home."

"Ignore Levi. He can be pushy."

Clint stared out the windshield. "I also have to get another coat on that scooter so I don't leave Brewster hanging."

Maria felt disappointed. Was this how Clint felt whenever something from back home intruded with her vacation?

Even though she knew the answer would be no, she asked, "Can you do it tomorrow?" He'd have all day before his late flight home.

He shook his head. "You know how it is."

"Sometimes being an adult is no fun." She held his hand over the console, admiring his features. He'd got a touch of sun across the bridge of his nose this week. "Hey, I've been hogging all your time. You didn't even get to go boogie boarding again, did you?"

"I'm actually rather grateful for that. Do you know how sorry I was the next day?"

"You were sore?"

He nodded.

"You hid it well."

"Good."

She laughed at his sincerity. "It's okay to be sore."

"Not when I keep going on about how our golden years will be our best." He gave a remorseful pout, and she laughed again. "Me hobbling around would defeat my entire argument."

She cupped his chin, loving the tenderness in his expression as her skin contacted his.

"I guess I better go up to the condo."

"You know, volunteers are notoriously flaky and flighty."

"They are?"

"Yeah, they never do half the jobs they sign up for."

She leaned back in the seat, toying with the suggestion of skipping her tasks. She glanced over at him again and found his hazel eyes were sparkling. "I don't think either of us has it in us to let our friends down tonight."

He chuckled and twisted his hands around the steering wheel. "You're probably right. I guess I'd better just ravage you with kisses and send you up there to paint some beautiful beach scenes. Maybe you can paint my initials into the clouds."

"You give my talent much more credit than it deserves."

"That's the part you focus on? I just told you I was going to ravage you with kisses."

"Oh, I mustn't have heard that. You know, when you're over the hill, first your hearing goes…"

"Get over here, old lady." Clint grabbed her by the elbow, pulling her closer. The first kiss missed her lips, landing on her cheek.

She giggled, shifting in the seat so the next kiss landed exactly where she wanted it. Right on her lips.

CHAPTER 8

The next morning Maria sat in a beach chair outside the Morrison Mansion Bed and Breakfast, admiring the crashing surf. Clint joined her with a cup of coffee in each hand.

Just one more day together. She had so much she wanted to talk about, as last night's painting session had opened up her mind to dreams and possibilities. So many ideas. And she knew she could share them with Clint. They could build something together. They really could.

He handed her a cup, not meeting her eyes.

"Are you going to the big football game?" she asked, taking a sip of her coffee. Tomorrow morning she'd fly directly to Dallas to watch the Sweetheart Creek high school football team battle for the title of state champions for their division. Two of her sons would be coaching, and the stands of the giant stadium would be filled with friends and family. Clint planned to fly home tonight, but she wasn't sure if he'd make the long drive to Dallas the very next day.

"I hope to, but I have some catching up to do." He winked

at her. "Some beach babe from Texas distracted me and suddenly my quick trip turned into a mini vacation."

Maria grimaced. Reality would hit them hard when they returned home. Chores and jobs were no doubt stacking up while, toes in the sand, they leisurely watched the sun crawl higher in the sky.

She shifted in her chair, hoping to shift the direction of her thoughts, too. "It is nice you could stay longer."

He reached across the space to squeeze her hand, his eyebrows raising.

"What?" she asked.

"You know you're important to me."

"Yes, you've said that."

"And what's important to you is important to me."

"You've said that, too." She set her cup in the sand. He was worrying her. "Are you okay?"

"Maria, I—"

"You ready?" It was Jeff, Clint's friend, coming up behind them, truck keys in hand.

"Where are you going?" Maria asked Clint.

"I have to leave." He set his cup down in the sand beside hers.

"I thought you were staying until tonight?" She tried to keep her voice level, but her heart betrayed her, making it wobble slightly.

"Something came up. I'm sorry."

Her surprise turned to annoyance. He'd just spent days pestering her about letting go and enjoying things. He'd made her feel guilty for enjoying how the ranch and her sons dominated her everyday life. He'd encouraged her to let loose, and then had turned around and secretly rebooked his flight to an earlier time?

What could have come up? Some broken-down cars? Couldn't his customers wait an extra few days? Yes, it was

Christmas and people wanted to go places, but the man deserved a holiday.

Just like she did.

They stood, Clint turning to her as Jeff retreated to his truck to wait.

"So now what?" Maria asked.

Yesterday she'd said they'd date back home, and now he was cutting his trip short. Was it because he'd gotten what he wanted?

Things were getting good, and now he was leaving.

It was difficult to not let that seep in and reopen old wounds.

"I'll see you in Sweetheart Creek?" he asked, squeezing her hand again. She pulled it back.

"The town has less than five thousand residents. It would be difficult not to." Her tone said it all. The hurt, the disappointment, the feeling of betrayal.

Clint shifted closer, his brows pinched. "I'm sorry. I know this is sudden. But trust me, it's important." He was looking at her as if she was supposed to understand, when he hadn't even given her details.

But she didn't understand. They didn't have enough history between them to bridge this moment. All she understood was that after a wonderful few days and a promise, he was suddenly turning around and leaving.

And she hadn't seen it coming.

MARIA WATCHED CLINT TAKE A FEW STEPS TOWARD THE TRUCK. He turned back, his eyes kind and seeking. "Please tell me you'll see me in Sweetheart Creek."

Unable to speak, she simply stood by the chairs and waited for him to leave.

He closed the distance between them again, his look so earnest she had to believe him when he said, "You're the one I've been waiting for, Maria."

And there was that out-of-control feeling she hated. He was getting serious, fast. Her chest tightened. Her heart battled her mind, and she didn't know what to think, say or feel.

He needed to slow down and take a deep breath. She'd agreed to go on a few dates back home to stave off boring evenings alone. She hadn't agreed to be the one he'd been waiting for.

She'd long ago left behind that heady hope of falling in love at the drop of a hat and believing it would all work out, and he knew that.

"We have too many miles behind us. How can you believe in an optimistic happily ever after? Especially based on such a quick whirlwind romance, or whatever this was?"

"Sometimes you just know." His hands reached for hers, gripping them.

He was so confident, so sure. But how long would that last?

"Haven't you ever just known?" he asked, his shaggy locks giving him a boyish vibe.

"What I've known is partnership. Roy was my focus for a long time, our lives entwined. Our love waned, but we still had what was important. We were in it together until the end." And then he'd changed his mind, fallen in love with someone new.

"That wasn't love, Maria. A partnership is very different from love."

"A partnership is what's left after the passion fades."

"Maybe if you're with the right person it stays on."

"My boys still need me," she whispered, extracting her hands from his.

"Your boys are fine. They're finding their own loves, their own lives."

"They need me on the ranch. They all lost a lot of weight when I was living in town. I take care of so many details."

"Being with me doesn't mean you have to give that up. What's important to you is important to me."

"Quit saying that! You know the ranch is my life."

"There's no room in your life for me? Is that what you're saying?" The hope and happiness she'd seen shining in his eyes faded. "Your sons seemed okay with me being around."

"They think you're wonderful, but they aren't ready for me to move on."

"Were they ready for Roy to do so?"

"It's different. I'm their mom."

Clint's frown showed he disagreed. She knew it was a weak argument, but it felt real. Men left. Women stayed, picked up the pieces and ensured the children didn't get too emotionally bashed in the wake of family turmoil.

"Maybe they're ready for you to live your own life. Have you thought of that? Have you tried talking to them like they're adults?"

His sharp tone of impatience was like a slap.

"I'm not using them as an excuse," she said sullenly.

"Then why don't you get to have a life? Why can't *you* find love?"

"It's not love." Her voice wobbled.

"What are you afraid of?" Clint asked. His tone was soothing, as though he was attempting to prevent a breakdown.

She was strong, though. Too strong to fall apart. She was strong enough to look out for herself and make tough decisions.

"Clint, I think you're special. I love spending time with

you, and our dates have been wonderful. You've brought me a lot of joy."

The muscles in his jaw tightened. "You've brought me a lot of joy, too."

"I don't think this is a good idea, however. I'm sorry."

"I love you, Maria." His jaw tightened with determination. "I'm not going anywhere."

"See? That's just it." A flash of anger, hot and searing, ripped through her. "Men leave, Clint. They make big promises and then they take off. You don't love me, because you don't know me. You think you do, but you don't. You say what's important to me is important to you. But you know what's important to me right now?" She pointed to the sand beneath her feet, her anger rising like the ocean waves. "Here? Today? You and me spending time together. That's important. And you're leaving. You're breaking your promise to me."

Clint inhaled slowly. She could see him contemplating what to say, how to talk her off this edge so he could stick to his plans.

"It's too fast, Clint. I'm not ready for this kind of stuff."

He swept his hands through his hair in frustration.

"I'm not ready for more hurt. I'm not ready to turn my life upside down for someone else." She crossed her arms, daring him to argue. "I told you we could see each other, but you're already breaking promises and assuming I'll just be here, all happy as a sideline thing."

"Maria…" The exasperation in his tone was new. He turned away with an exhalation, then swung back to her, his tone more patient. "Maria, you're more than a sideline thing. Can you believe that? Could you believe for one minute that maybe I'm not leaving you?"

"Funny, because you're about to get on a plane. That's

called leaving. You're going home twelve hours before you said you were."

"Hours, Maria. Mere hours."

She crossed her arms once more. He couldn't talk her out of this. Her husband had left, her father had left. Even her son Cole had left, and was barely in contact. She couldn't take more heartbreak. Couldn't take more promises of love and devotion, just to have it all ripped away. She needed someone who would be there every single step. Clint had made her believe she was important, and this sure didn't show it.

"I thought I was worth more than some fears to you," he said. "I guess I was wrong."

He began walking toward the truck, and Maria could've sworn he took a piece of her heart with him. A piece she hadn't realized still existed.

OF COURSE HER FEARS HAD PLAYED A ROLE IN THINGS. JUST AS Clint's had. He'd moved too fast. How could either of them know if this was love? He hadn't even told her why he was leaving. And yet he expected her to trust him and understand?

How had their lovely morning on the beach turned so foul so quickly?

Maria emptied their coffee cups and set them on the steps leading up to the bed-and-breakfast. She walked back to Kit's condo, lost in her thoughts like she'd gotten lost in painting the gala's canvas bags last night, her hopes and dreams for the future building with each brushstroke. In all her thoughts Clint had played a starring role. Ideas had come to her on how she could give her sons more space, leave herself more time to enjoy the finer side of life with Clint and friends.

Hobbies, travel possibilities and more. She'd been ready to live life to the fullest.

And now this.

How could he just leave?

What was so vital back home?

He kept saying that what was important to her was important to him.

Her sons and the ranch were important, but he wouldn't be going back for that. There was nothing for him other than to fix the stupid tractor. And that wasn't at all urgent. Him spending time here, with her… That was important.

He made no sense.

At least with Roy she'd understood why he'd left.

And saying he loved her? Had Clint not been listening to her all week? She needed to go slow. She'd agreed to one thing, and when she'd turned around he was practically on bended knee, proposing.

She stormed into Kit's apartment and kicked off her shoes. She stopped in front of the table in the kitchen nook, her eyes catching on the canvas bags.

She picked one up and studied it critically. Maria wanted to crumple it in her hands, throw it in the corner and stomp on it. Instead, she inspected it while sinking into a chair.

The painting wasn't half-bad. Not the most original art, but nice. With good detail.

Nonthreatening.

She'd never be an artist, but as a hobby, painting was a fine one.

She stacked the dried bags and wondered if Clint had finished the scooter. It was so unlike him to up and leave. Or maybe she didn't truly know him.

She sorted the paintbrushes and supplies. In one of her dreams last night, she'd imagined herself all decked out for the gala. Clint had been wearing a tuxedo, and she'd been so happy. In her dream, the night had been unlike anything from her real life. She'd chatted with the movie star Eric Slade, listened to Ariana Carol's beautiful singing, and hung out with the town's mayor, Amanda Strickland, and many others.

Moving to Kit's guest room, Maria began packing up the things she wouldn't need before tomorrow morning's flight to Dallas. Instead of living her grand fantasy, she was flying home to support her boys and their football team.

She wouldn't give up her family for anything, but she still felt a strange sense of loss for what might have been if the timing had been better with the gala and Clint.

Maria stood at the bedroom window and blindly stared outside, wondering what her future would bring beyond chores, family and routine. Would she find love again? Real love. Not what Clint thought he had.

How would she handle bumping into him around town? It was going to be so awkward.

Pulling herself out of the daze, Maria moved to the stack of finished bags outside her bedroom. She smoothed her hand over one where she'd painted a palm tree bending in the wind. Clint had revived something in her, and even if she couldn't have him, she decided she'd keep what he'd restored within her.

With her jaw set, Maria grabbed her purse. There was one more thing she had to do before she left Indigo Bay.

She arrived at Seaside Cycles out of breath, her mind whirling with inspiration. She collected an airbrush kit from one of the shop assistants, Liam. He gave her a few tips, then watched as she tested it out. Satisfied she wouldn't destroy the scooter, he turned her loose. She attacked the scooter, praying she didn't mar its perfect paint job with her own additions.

Two hours later she stretched the kinks out of her back

and admired her work. Not flawless by any means, but her custom painting was raw and full of life.

A deliriously happy, fat mermaid settled herself on a rock as waves crashed around her, mid-storm. She looked strong, and somehow slightly surly.

It was perfect.

And then Maria began to cry.

Out on the street, she collected herself and called the one person she knew would understand. The one person who could help her sort through the confusion and pain that was making her heart ache like it never had before.

"He said what?" Fiona said into the phone, so loudly that Maria lifted her cell away from her ear and lowered the volume. Fiona's voice mellowed as she said to someone in the diner, "I'm on the phone. You can wait for a top-up."

"I can call back later," Maria offered.

"No, you called me at the diner, which means it's important. Garfield can wait for more coffee." She said it firmly, as though daring the old man to argue with her.

"Way to lay down the law," Maria said with a chuckle.

"It's the only way to handle the opposite sex. Show them who's boss." There was a sassy flirtatiousness to her tone, and Maria wondered what her friend was playing with. She knew things weren't good with her husband, William, but Fiona wasn't the type to step out on her marriage. Not even for the persistent and sweet Garfield, a man half the town was rooting for.

"Clint wants to get serious. He's saying he knows I'm the one for him."

"And?" There was a tremor of excitement in Fiona's voice.

"What do you mean, and? We were supposed to be having

fun, enjoying some adventures, and now he's getting serious and acting as though I need to change my life for him." Her voice grew louder, and she lowered it even though there was nobody sharing the empty sidewalk in front of Seaside Cycles.

"I understand," Fiona said smoothly. "You've centered your life around others for a long time. You definitely don't want anyone in your family to be inconvenienced by you taking what you want for once."

"Exactly!" Maria said, before pausing. "What?"

"People will be inconvenienced if you follow your heart and date Clint. Your boys will have to get over the fact that you, too, have a life, and that includes having wants and needs."

Maria shut her eyes. Her friend was twisting things around.

"Moving on is hard," Fiona said. "I understand that. It takes courage. You know some folks will be unhappy if you follow your heart, and they'll be unhappy if you don't."

Maria had a feeling her friend was talking about her own situation with her bear of a husband.

"What if you follow your heart and make everyone unhappy? And then it doesn't even work out because you were rushing into things?" Maria said.

"Valid point. You could lose either way. But sometimes you have to take what you need and tell everyone else to go to—" There was a crash. "Oops. Dropped some plates."

"I should let you go."

"No, it's fine. They're not going to get any worse than they already are now—broken."

"Why can't this be easy?" Maria's heart ached and her eyes welled with tears.

"Because you're used to being the good wife, the good

mom, the good rancher, the good friend. It's natural for you to put others first."

Maria sighed. She'd been hearing that a lot lately.

"Maybe it's time to switch your priorities," Fiona said.

"It's not about that," Maria said. Putting herself first would no doubt make her feel selfish and greedy.

She caught herself. That was *really* twisted, and she'd scold her friends if she caught them thinking that way. What was the worst that would happen if she grabbed what she wanted and let everyone deal with their own emotional fallout?

"Do you think your ex-husband agonized over dating Sophia the way you are with Clint? I bet he thought something along the lines of this being his one life and wanting to live it the way he wanted to. He decided to do what makes him happy."

"He was a selfish jerk," Maria said, her heart thrumming with anger. "The way he acted was completely inconsiderate." He'd thrown so much away, caused such upheaval and hurt. She couldn't be like that.

"He broke your heart, in order to make two hearts happy. That's not bad math."

"But it was wrong." Maria winced, biting her lip to help focus her thoughts. But was it? Would she rather he'd stayed with her even though their love was gone and he was thinking about someone else? That would have been a different kind of wrong, and quite possibly more awful.

"Are you gonna take some action, or are you gonna sit at home and break your own heart as well as Clint's because you think you don't deserve love?"

"It's not about deserving love." Just saying that filled her with longing. With Clint she felt special and cherished. It was nice having someone ask what she wanted. Nice putting her needs first sometimes—even if they were frivolous and trivial.

"How do you think your grown-up boys would feel if they knew you hadn't accepted someone's love and had lived out your remaining days as a lonely old thing because you believed they weren't mature enough to handle it? Did you not raise men who care about others?"

"This isn't about them."

"It is if you're using them as an excuse."

Maria sighed at the logic. How was it that Kit, Clint and Fiona were all echoing each other this week when they argued with her? Was her perspective on things really that muddled?

"I suggest you sit on that beautiful beach with a glass of wine and get yourself sorted out. Clint's been waiting for you for a very long time, and if you push him away, he might just decide he's going to go find love somewhere else."

"He already did."

"What?"

"He left."

"I thought his flight was for tonight."

"It was."

"Why? Why did he change it? Was this before or after his… proclamation?"

"He didn't say why and he changed it before."

"Garfield! Yeah, you. No, I don't have coffee. I'm still on the phone. Why did Clint change his flight home?"

Fiona was quiet for a moment, listening to Garfield. Then she said to Maria, "He doesn't know. But that poor mechanic has been pining over a married woman for a decade. Pining, Maria," Fiona said firmly. "Do you hear me? He took his chance and my guess is that you got scared and shut it down and so he retreated."

"He didn't just retreat. He *left* me."

"Don't be so dramatic. He didn't leave you. You know where he is." She lowered her voice. "Maria?"

"Yeah?"

"He's a good man."

"I know."

"He'll walk out that door forever and leave you your space if that's what you ask for." Fiona let that sink in. "So you need to sit down and think real hard about what you want and what you're afraid of before it's too late. You hear?"

Maria sighed in reply.

"Go get that glass of wine and think. Then call me once you've made your decision about this man. And know that if it's not the right one, I'm gonna march all the way to Indigo Bay and set your head on straight."

The firmness in her friend's voice made Maria smile. "You're the best friend a woman could ask for, Fiona."

"No one can dish it like I can." Her voice became stern as she addressed somebody on the other end of the line. "Garfield, get up off your knee. You're being ridiculous." She gave a worldly sigh. "I'm a married woman and my advice was for Maria, not me, not you."

"Maybe it's advice you should take, too," Maria said. But the line had already gone dead, leaving her with nothing but her friend's words repeating in her head.

CHAPTER 9

Several days after the state championship game Maria sat in the spacious kitchen at the Sweet Meadows Ranch, a fresh cup of peppermint tea in front of her. She wasn't thirsty, but she liked the smell of peppermint when she was feeling out of sorts. She had boxes of tea in her miniature home out in the yard, but the idea of being alone in the cramped space felt as though it would only amplify what she was feeling right now.

She wanted to talk to Clint. She'd half expected him to come to the championship game, half expected him to show up at her door at some point. But he hadn't, and there had been no texts, no calls.

Fiona was right. Maria had made it clear she didn't have room for him in her life, and now he was respecting that by staying out of it.

It made her want to grab him and run away to Indigo Bay so they could return to that glorious bubble they'd created.

He was a wonderful man. His kisses divine. And she wasn't going to kid herself any longer. Clint had been fun. He'd been exactly what she'd needed and had brought her so much joy. And to be honest, it had been refreshing having someone looking out for her for once.

Hearing the soft footfalls of sneakers, she waited for her youngest son, Ryan, to appear in the kitchen. He'd been spending more time on the ranch in the past few days, partly, she suspected, to distract himself from his own life and its ups and downs.

"Hey, Mom." He sat at the long table. "What's happening?"

She asked him about himself, his team, Carly, but it wasn't long before he asked about Clint and Indigo Bay. Word of their time together had traveled quickly in Sweetheart Creek.

She dodged Ryan's questions, giving him a "Clint and I are friends" response.

"He's made it clear he'd like to be more than that."

"Have you been talking to Levi?" She sat straighter and clutched her cup.

"You don't like Clint?"

"He is a very thoughtful man who…" She clucked, catching herself. "You don't want to hear about your mother's love life."

"You have a love life?"

She narrowed her eyes. No wonder so many of Ryan's students came to him for advice. She'd seen it before and after football games, and now she understood why. He had a way about him.

"Tell me," he said, reminding her of Clint.

"Why don't you tell me about you and Carly instead?"

Ryan deftly tried to change the subject, just like she had. Her youngest kept his cards close to his chest, and usually was a distracted, fast-moving missile. He kept his hands in several projects at a time, his head always somewhere else. But right now he looked like he could use a cookie and a glass of milk. And maybe a hug, too.

Something had definitely happened with Carly. And seeing as the tractor was still around, she had a feeling his plan to help out the independent woman had fallen through.

Maria opened her mouth to speak, then closed it, knowing it was time to let her sons do more of their own problem solving. They were good at it.

Before she realized it, they were arguing mildly about whether men or women broke up more relationships.

"Women leave," Ryan said.

Maria laughed. He was wrong.

She sobered quickly. Had Carly left him?

"*Men* leave. I guess women do, too," she said finally. "People leave."

Maybe it was truly that simple, just one of those facts of life. People were born. People died. Sometimes they left others. Sometimes they didn't.

Clint hadn't left Kay-Lynn. She'd left him.

And maybe sometimes women *should* leave, like Fiona, but they didn't. Her friend kept hanging on to William, refusing to let him go, refusing to let his new attitude defeat them and their love.

"You gave it a shot with Clint, didn't you?" Ryan asked.

"I tried, but he left," Maria said absently, still sorting out her thoughts about Fiona and William.

"He *left*?" Ryan asked with a hint of incredulity.

She explained how he'd flown home early.

"So he up and went home?"

Before long they were talking about Brant and April, Cole and everyone under the sun, it seemed. Ryan reminded her so much of that little boy who'd once sought her advice. He hadn't asked her for much in so long it broke her heart, thinking how independent her youngest had become.

Then suddenly, while she was putting her cup in the dishwasher, Ryan said, "You know he came home because Levi needed him to?"

He mentioned the tractor, but she knew that wasn't the real reason Clint had returned. It didn't add up. Clint had been like Fiona, steadfastly clinging to love and hope, and everything they'd built over those four days together. Plus the tractor was still out of commission, and if he'd come back early as a gesture to show he was worthy of her heart, then why hadn't he at least called?

There was still a missing piece to the whole Clint puzzle.

"I know you worry about how Clint would fit into our lives, but do you think Dad cared when he married Sophia? Maybe you need to take care of yourself for once." Ryan stood, such certainty in his posture. "I don't think Clint left you, Mom. I think you're seeing what you want to see out of fear of getting hurt."

Her son was right, but she wasn't sure where to go from here. She'd never had to deal with anything like this with Roy. It had always been straightforward. Never charged with such emotion.

She'd said some things to Clint that had made it clear she didn't want him in her life.

And she had been so very wrong.

"Is Clint here?" Maria stood at the back counter and scanned the Longhorn Diner, not seeing the man in question. Christmas songs played over the speakers, and in a few days the holiday would have come and gone. She still needed to sort something out with Roy regarding Christmas Day. He and the boys had all been leaning toward having their own celebration the day after, and she kept her fingers crossed it would all work out for them. "Jenny from the shop next door said she saw him come in."

"I know who Jenny Oliver is," Fiona said with an amused smirk. "You just missed him."

Maria slid onto a stool, giving the room a second glance. In one of the booths, Carly Clarke was sitting with Laura, April and Jackie. They were huddled together, chatting.

But no Clint.

"Did he get the tractor fixed?" Fiona asked.

"I don't think so," Maria said distractedly.

Her friend leaned against the counter. "For the record, I'm still not impressed about you not fixing things with him. But you looking for him has promise. I heard he's going to Riverbend to pick up a part. He was in here getting coffee to go."

Maria stood.

"He's already long gone," Fiona warned.

It felt like she'd been chasing him for days and was always missing him. Coincidence? Likely, but she was getting paranoid that he might be avoiding her, and she wasn't sure how much longer her courage would last when it came to trying to track him down to talk about things.

"Something's up," Maria said, feeling as though everyone had been a bit more guarded since she'd come home.

"Yeah?" Fiona's eyebrows lifted. "Like what?"

"I'm not sure. Do you know?" She studied her friend, on the lookout for a hint or a tell.

Fiona picked up her coffeepot. "I've got to take the girls a top-up."

Maria turned, surprised she was letting the topic drop. Was Fiona a part of whatever was making everyone slightly weird lately, or had Maria really shifted her perspective while away and now everything and everyone seemed different to her?

"Karen'll want coffee." Fiona pointed toward the town's librarian, who'd joined Carly's table.

The diner was fairly busy for a Wednesday, and Maria impatiently waited for Fiona to return. She finally slipped behind the counter to make a fresh pot of coffee, saying, "You never told me how the gala went."

"Kit said there were some hiccups and drama, of course, but otherwise it went well, as did the adoption drive. They raised enough money to expand the animal shelter after a generous last-minute donation came in."

"And your paintings on the bags were popular, I heard?"

"It sounds like they were a nice added touch."

"And Clint's scooter?"

Maria had to look away. "Kit said it brought in a lot."

"I knew it would. And you heard Travis is wondering if you'll paint a mural for the town?" Fiona asked, referring to the mayor, Travis Nestner.

"I think his triplets would do a better job of it. Or at least Donna. She's got some creativity and talent." His wife had designed the logo for Brant's vet clinic, Call of the Wyld(er).

It was nice having a hobby again, but she definitely wasn't ready to take on a mural.

Fiona perked up, saying, "Oh, there's Clint! He's talking with Levi."

"What?" Maria turned to look, then spun back to the counter. She couldn't talk to him. Not here.

"Oh, now they're leaving with Brant."

Maria forced herself not to react. "Is this all really about a tractor?" And why were her boys working with Clint so much? Were they okay with him, but only if she wasn't dating him?

"It's so busy right now with Christmas a few days away. Why don't you wait and talk to Clint on the weekend?" Fiona poked at her hair, making the Christmas-colored gems entwined in it sparkle.

"I like your hairdo."

"I know. Everyone does."

Her friend flitted off again and Maria sat, thinking. Was Clint really that busy? Why else would Fiona suggest Maria wait to talk to him?

CHAPTER 10

On Christmas Day Maria entered the living room to tell her boys and their loved ones that supper was ready. Roy and Sophia would have dinner with them tomorrow, letting Maria have them all to herself today, a real Christmas gift.

Gratitude.

So much to be grateful for. Her boys were finding love. Ryan and Carly had seemingly fixed whatever had occurred between them, and Laura and Levi were curled up together like Myles and Karen were. She'd even caught Brant and April looking at each other in a special way. The only son missing was Cole.

Her new dog, a rescue found by Brant, leaned against her leg and she absently bent and gave Bingo a reassuring scratch behind the ears. He'd been such a skinny mess when he'd arrived a few days ago, but was already looking healthier.

The front door opened, and something inside her stilled. She turned, her nerve endings firing both flames, then ice. For a moment she couldn't speak, couldn't even gasp.

It was Cole. Her second born had returned home after five long years away. Her feet ate up the ground between them and she threw her arms around him. For long moments Maria held him tightly, unable to believe he was truly here.

The wish she'd made on that Christmas tree ornament had come true, even though she'd broken the Indigo Bay tradition. How did that already feel like months ago, when it had been only last week?

"Hey, Mom," Cole said, after the excited hubbub had died down, his brothers had welcomed him home. "I hope I'm not late for supper."

She just shook her head, still speechless. He said it so casually, as though he'd merely stepped out to take care of some chores before the meal. Not run off without a word five endless years ago.

"You're never too late," she said, her voice almost failing her.

He held her gaze, and she scanned him. He was broader, and looked more sure of himself, but had a shadow in his eyes she knew meant he would need some time to heal from what had driven him away. Away from her. Away from family. Away from home.

It wasn't until everyone began moving toward the kitchen that the shock began to wear off. And as it did she caught sight of someone else familiar standing in the doorway.

Clint Walker.

Once again something inside her stilled, and then began to thrum.

Without thinking, she took several steps his way. The living room and entry area had cleared out, leaving them alone.

Clint had been wearing a cowboy hat, and he lowered it to his chest. "Merry Christmas, Maria."

His eyes didn't leave hers, taking in details.

He was clutching a box about the size of a softball in his free hand. "I thought you might like this," he said, holding it out.

She stepped forward, accepting the box. It was light. "What is it?" She opened the flap and saw a Christmas ornament nestled in tissue paper, the one with her seascape painted on it. Almost flabbergasted, she looked up at him. "You kept it?" Then the artist in her had to study the scene. Her seascape wasn't so bad. Here in Texas, it brought her nothing but warm memories of laughing with Clint while painting, going for scooter rides, and walking around town.

Lots of good, good memories. She hugged the ornament to her chest.

"Thank you, Clint." He'd brought it home for her without saying a word, as if knowing that, given time, she might cherish the item and all it represented.

"I heard about your mermaid."

"On the scooter?" Her cheeks heated thinking about the anger-fueled airbrush job.

He nodded, his gaze not leaving hers. "I hope you'll keep doing things you enjoy."

Before she could summon a reply, her five boys—all five!—came hurrying back into the room, Levi in the lead. "Mom! We almost forgot," he told her.

"Forgot what?" she asked, turning to face them. Their eyes were smiling and their faces glowing like their dad's used to when he was their age. They were happy. All of them.

"We have a surprise," Levi announced.

She glanced at Cole, who gave a shrug and a smile.

"No, Cole isn't our surprise," Brant said solemnly, clapping his taller brother on the shoulder.

"Great. Now supper's going to be late," Carmichael grumbled, crossing his arms. Despite his tone, his lips twitched showing he wasn't truly upset.

The boys kept darting quick looks in Clint's direction, but before Maria could sort anything out, Levi was hustling her toward the door, Myles on her other side.

"You brought it, right?" Levi asked Clint as they shuffled Maria out onto the front porch.

"Sure did," Clint replied, his voice so low and quiet it almost seemed as though he wanted to fade into the background.

"What are you boys up to?" Maria asked, anticipation swirling in her gut. They hadn't given her a gift to open that morning, telling her one would arrive later.

Cole was here, but he wasn't the gift. Clint was here, but he wasn't, either, but he was somehow connected.

So what was it?

Several strong hands turned her to face the gravel driveway. To the right of the porch was a familiar red car.

Her Mustang.

It was no longer coated in dust or cobwebs, but its Candy Apple body had been buffed, washed and waxed, and looked beautiful.

She took a few steps down off the porch to take a better look, then turned back to the boys with a questioning glance. They all smiled and turned toward Clint. His expression gave nothing away.

She walked to the car, trailed her fingers along the body.

"Sorry about the timing," Clint said, appearing beside her with the boys. "I meant to get it here before suppertime."

"One of the last parts came in yesterday," Levi said.

"You were right. I should've ordered them sooner," Clint said to him.

Levi had clapped a hand on Clint's shoulder and was

leaning against him. "But you got it done, and it looks amazing."

Maria studied the Mustang. "You fixed the engine and that stalling issue?" she asked.

Levi launched into a diatribe, listing all the things Clint had done on the vehicle once they'd told him their Christmas plan. He'd not only spruced it up, he'd made the car reliable and roadworthy once again.

Kittim's words about buying a new car if things failed with her and Clint ran through Maria's head. Except now she had a car that was older than her grown boys and would surely need regular mechanical intervention to keep it on the road. And if she didn't take care of it, her sons would be hurt and disappointed.

"Merry Christmas, Mom," Myles exclaimed. He wrapped his arm around her shoulders and pulled her close.

"She's speechless again," Carmichael called from the front porch.

"Do you want to take it for a spin?" Clint asked.

"But supper's ready," she answered, unable to look away from the car.

"You don't get surprises often, do you?" he whispered.

She glanced around, realizing that all the other women, no doubt knowing about the big surprise, had stayed inside and were likely keeping the food warm.

"No worries. That's being taken of," Clint confirmed, as though reading her mind. He held up her old key chain, dangling it.

She took it and grinned. A feeling of freedom, joy and adventure ripped through her.

"We thought you could use some fun wheels again as you venture into the next phase of life," Brant said.

"But we're not calling you old," Myles said quickly.

Maria opened the driver's side door, noting the old

familiar squeak was no longer there. She sank into the seat, expecting a musty smell. Instead, the interior gleamed, fresh and renewed.

Biting her bottom lip, she tentatively turned the key. The engine roared to life, just like the old scooter had back in Indigo Bay. Clint had a way with taking the worn and used and making them new again.

Just like her.

MARIA WAS STILL REELING FROM HAVING COLE HOME AND HAD reached over more than once during the meal to give his arm a squeeze, as if making sure he was real. Each time, he'd smile, but the last time he asked if she was okay.

"Yes. It's just so lovely to have you home." She stopped herself from asking how long he would stay.

She found her gaze trailing down the table to where Clint was sitting near Carmichael. It sounded as though they were talking about diesel engines.

Clint must have felt her watching him, for he turned her way with a smile. How involved in all of her surprises was he? The car, for sure. But Cole's arrival? Had he done that, too? Was that silly old car what had pulled him home from Indigo Bay? Was that why Levi had been fretting about ordering parts?

"The tractor was a decoy, wasn't it?" she asked Levi.

He smiled.

He'd never planned to get it running again, but used it as something to keep her off the trail of their surprise.

If he only knew she would have rather had Clint with her for one more day in Indigo Bay. She watched Clint eat and laugh with her father-in-law, wondering when she'd have a chance to speak with him. The fact that he'd stayed for supper suggested she was still important to him and he hoped for a second chance.

Realizing she was off in her own world, she turned to Cole. "So, how did you know…"

"Know what?" he asked.

"That I wanted…" She shook her head. "I forgot what I was going to say."

Clint had been watching her again. He said, loudly enough for her to hear, but not enough to interrupt the various conversations going on around the table, "It seemed important to you." His gaze flickered to Cole.

He'd brought her son home. For her.

Brant had reached out to Cole several times over the years. But judging by his shocked, pale face and the way he kept giving his brother wary glances, she knew he hadn't called Cole home this time. Not when he was making eyes at Cole's ex-girlfriend and helping her regain her footing in life after divorce.

And Levi, her take-charge eldest, had tried to get hold of him back in the fall, but Cole had never picked up his calls. Myles and Ryan were a no, as well.

"You didn't tell him I'm dying, did you?" she asked Clint, curious how he'd managed to get her son to return home.

"What? You're dying?" Ryan turned to her, his eyes huge.

"No!" She lifted a hand, laughing. "No, I'm fine."

Clint chuckled and shook his head.

"He said you needed me," Cole interjected, when everyone at the table went back to their earlier conversations.

"Oh, I…" She wasn't comfortable putting that kind of weight or pressure on her son. She wanted him to return home because he wished to, not because he'd been guilted into it or felt obligated.

"It was a good excuse," Cole said with that mischievous

smile of his. That hadn't changed. He'd always been a bit of a brat. In the best way. Except for when it got him into trouble. Her gaze automatically tracked to April and her young son, Kurt.

Cole cracked a joke. "Come on, Mom. Everyone knows you don't need anyone."

That used to feel true.

"Time for dessert?" Myles asked hopefully, from farther down the table.

"You're still hungry?" Cole asked incredulously.

"Always."

"I would have thought you'd have outgrown that phase," Cole said, standing to help clear the table.

"Nope. Not yet." Myles stretched his strong body, showing his flat stomach. Hard work on the ranch followed by coaching his football team kept him trim.

"I've got to get the pies from the cold room," Maria said, not expecting anyone to respond.

Clint half stood, but Cole said, "I'll help."

In the basement, Maria loaded two pies into Cole's hands, then picked up two as well.

"What are you going to do about April?" she asked him. Brant was finally having his moment with her, but Maria knew that could get blown up by Cole's arrival.

"What about her?"

"Well, you're home and…"

"I was waiting for her to call me, but I don't think she'll ever be ready for my return. So… Here I am."

"What happened between the two of you? Really happened?" Maria had plenty of assumptions and had heard the town's own speculation, but she'd never heard the entire story straight from the horse's mouth.

Her son exhaled, his chest expanding. "Dad thought…" He shook his head.

"Roy? What did he do?" Sudden anger roared in her ears. "Did he send you away?"

There'd been the fight before Cole had left, but she hadn't thought Roy had actually told him to leave town.

"I'm here now."

Her shoulder sagged. "Your dad and I have very different views on things, and I hope you can stay. You're always welcome here on the ranch. This will always be your home."

"Thanks." He gave her a soft smile. "I've missed this place."

"It's missed you, too. We all have."

"Yeah, Levi's already asking me which chores I want to do in the morning." He grinned and Maria shook her head at the familiar argument between her sons.

"So what's this about you and Clint?" Cole asked. "I was surprised when he called me up."

"He phoned you?" she said, wanting to hear more.

"Yeah, he said it was important for me to come home for Christmas." There was a hesitation in his voice and she hurried to assure Cole that his arrival was welcomed.

"It was. It is! I'm so glad you've come and I'm sorry I haven't called you sooner and asked."

"I needed some time. And I think April did, too."

"But this is your home."

"It's also hers."

It was. She'd been raised here like a Wylder. And that was half the issue with Cole's return. Could they all figure things out now that there was so much water under the bridge?

"You're a good man," Maria told him.

"I try." They were still standing in the cold room, pies in hand. "So you and Clint? Are you a thing? Dad's remarried, right?"

"He and Sophia are doing well. They're living in town and your brothers and Carmichael are going over there tomorrow for supper. I'm sure they'd be happy to see you."

"And you? Have you moved on?" Cole asked, ignoring her attempt at a subject change.

"I have not." She gave him a look that said she didn't want to discuss the subject.

"Clint really likes you."

She made a noncommittal sound.

"Mom!" Cole's voice had a commanding note that had her focusing on him again. "How many times did Brant try to convince me to come home? He even tracked me down in Blueberry Springs, and I still never came. Not even for Dad's wedding."

Maria sighed. Of course he hadn't come back for Roy. Not after the way he'd left.

"Clint made a very compelling argument about you wanting me home. He made points that could only be made by someone really close to you, Mom. Someone you'd shared things with."

"It's not like that," she said gruffly. But she was starting to see that it was. She'd shared her deepest worries and fears about Cole and her role in his absence. And Clint had listened, then lent a hand to patch up things in a way that even Brant had failed.

"I've forgiven Dad, you know," Cole said.

She gave him a sharp, assessing look. "You have?"

"Yeah."

"Well, I don't think I have. Not for scaring you off for almost five years."

"Well, that's a long story," Cole said, hinting that she might not know all of it.

"Hey, did you guys get lost, or are you keeping all the pie for yourselves?" Clint appeared around the corner with a grin on his craggy face.

Cole tipped his head toward the man, giving Maria a

secret smile while scooting from the room. "Mom could use your help."

"Let me take one of those," Clint said, stepping forward.

She shivered as his hand touched hers as he slid the apple pie from her grip, leaving her the blueberry.

"Still mad at me?" he asked.

"I don't know what to be," she admitted.

"How about being in love with me?" He winked, and she laughed despite herself. What was it about this man, anyway?

"Why did you leave Indigo Bay? What was so important?" she finally asked him.

"You haven't figured it out yet?"

"I want to hear it straight from you."

"Levi needed help with the tractor."

"Nope." She knew it was more than some silly old decoy tractor that had brought him home.

"Well, I did say I'd take a look at it. We were secretly restoring the Mustang for you. I needed to get back to finish the project so the boys could give it to you on Christmas Day."

"And?"

"I had to pick up Cole from the airport this afternoon."

"So let me get this straight..." She studied him for a moment, his heavenly brown eyes never leaving hers. "You cut short your time with me in order to help my boys, and you brought Cole home?"

"He paid for his own ticket."

Maria was silent for a long moment. The man was very forgivable, and he'd done an amazing job of showing her that what was important to her was important to him.

Except for that silly car. She'd have taken even one more hour with him on the beach in exchange for her Mustang. Even though it was a pretty sweet ride. And she supposed it wasn't about the car, it was about the fact that he'd left her to help her sons do something special for her.

"Merry Christmas?" he murmured, his voice lifting with hope.

As she set their pies back down on the shelf so she could wrap him in her arms, she had a feeling that their mutual hope was the basis of all future joy.

aria was glad she was the one driving. She was nervous and excited, and driving gave her something to do with her hands. She and Clint were officially going on their first Sweetheart Creek date. And it wasn't just meeting up for coffee and dessert, or having supper one town over, or even hiding out together in a darkened movie theater.

They were going to a community barn dance. And not just any barn dance, but the New Year's Eve one, which was the biggest night of the year. Guaranteeing a kiss at midnight, which was like claiming Clint Walker as her man for the entire New Year.

New year. New life.

Not really a new life, but one with more pauses to enjoy what came her way, even something as simple as sitting on the porch swing with Clint and listening to the birds sing. A life with more kisses.

She smiled and glanced over at him, the car's dash lights emphasizing his features. She was driving her restored

Mustang, the feel of the machine so familiar it was like coming home.

Kind of like Clint. He already felt like an integral part of her life, her home, her world. He'd been hanging around the ranch a bit since Christmas Day, popping in here and there. Sometimes he'd stop for a morning coffee if the post-Christmas rush at Clint's Parts and Mechanic wasn't too bad, other times for a game of cards after supper, or simply a quick lunch.

The boys approved of Clint. Pulling him in to help with their Christmas surprise, and him bringing Cole home had solidified him as a member of the Wylder clan.

The future hadn't been something to worry about, after all.

As she parked behind the old barn converted into a community center a few miles from town, and shut off the engine, country-and-western music immediately reached their ears. She turned to Clint and, as though he'd read her mind, he leaned across the console, his minty breath brushing her cheek. He cupped her chin, bringing her in for a lingering kiss that made her toes curl in anticipation and joy.

"Will you kiss me at midnight?" she whispered.

"And tomorrow. And the next day."

She shifted in her seat. "So what are we doing here?" She knew she wanted something serious with Clint. Not marriage, at least not yet. But something long-term and solid. Something they could both rely on.

"Is your memory going? We were kissing." He pulled her in for another one, his body warm and welcoming. She'd missed him in the few days they hadn't seen each other, and it all seemed so foolish and fear-driven now.

"I like the way we're taking it slow," she murmured, "but I know you want more."

"I do. But I also learned that I'd prefer the agony of taking it slow over not having you at all."

"Oh, Clint." She tugged at his jacket, pulling him close enough for another kiss.

"You're worth waiting for," he said, brushing her smeared lipstick with a rough thumb. "By the way, I think your boys like me."

"You've won them over."

"And Carmichael doesn't seem to mind me on the ranch as long as I'm willing to talk about diesel engines."

"When you tire of that, he also likes to discuss bulls."

Her father-in-law didn't seem to mind having a new man around the ranch in his son's place. Maria shouldn't have sold him short. Carmichael was a widower and likely understood the loneliness, and the need to move on. He hadn't said a word about Clint, but she'd noted he'd started calling her a young filly here and there. And whenever he saw Maria and Clint laughing or cuddling, she could have sworn she'd see a glimmer of a smile tease the old cowboy's lips.

They exited the car, and as they walked toward the barn Maria slipped her hand into Clint's. "I'm looking forward to a lot of things because of you."

"What kind of things?"

"Taking it easy. Being myself. Pursuing my interests— while still helping on the ranch."

"Of course. That's a big part of who you are."

"It is. And you know, I thought it would be weird having you around on the ranch, but it isn't."

"It's been okay?" She heard the hesitation in his voice.

She squeezed his hand. "It's been more than okay. Life adapts. I'd forgotten that."

"It does, doesn't it?"

"Thank you, Clint."

"I'm not sure what you're thanking me for."

"For not giving up, and for pushing me. Your persistence was needed."

"It's what I do best. But Maria?" He stopped, pulling her hand to bring her back to him.

"Yeah?"

"I should confess that it was for purely selfish reasons."

She smiled and nestled into his side. "Yeah?"

"I didn't want anyone else getting to you before I had a chance."

"Is that so?"

"It is."

"I couldn't imagine being with anyone else." She realized it was the truth. "And I'm glad you came to Indigo Bay."

"Are you two coming in?" Myles called from the open doorway. It was a cool night, and they'd set up the donation table for the barn's upkeep inside instead of out in front like usual. Myles had one hand on the door, ready to close it if they said no.

They began hurrying across the grassy area. "We're coming!"

Myles saw their linked hands and his smile grew. He nudged Levi and Ryan, who were standing with him. They turned, and smiled in tandem. Right then Maria knew without a doubt that absolutely everything would turn out exactly the way it was meant to be.

THANK YOU FOR READING SWEET JOYMAKER. I HOPE YOU enjoyed Maria and Clint's Christmas story about finding love again. Do Maria's five boys find love? Find out what happens in Maria and Clint's hometown of Sweetheart Creek, Texas! Start reading *The Cowboys of Sweetheart Creek,*

Texas series with Levi's book, **THE COWBOY'S STOLEN HEART.**

And there's more Indigo Bay, too! The next book in the series is SWEET YULETIDE by Melissa McClone! Find what Indigo Bay has in store for Sheridan and Mikey this holiday season!

MORE FROM INDIGO BAY!

Indigo Bay Second Chance Romances

Sweet Troublemaker (Book 1) by Jean Oram

Sweet Do-Over (Book 2) by Melissa McClone

Sweet Horizons (Book 3) by Jean C. Gordon

Sweet Complications (Book 4) by Stacy Claflin

Sweet Whispers (Book 5) by Jeanette Lewis

Sweet Adventure (Book 6) by Tamie Dearen

Indigo Bay Sweet Romance Series

Sweet Dreams (Book 1) by Stacy Claflin

Sweet Matchmaker (Book 2) by Jean Oram

Sweet Sunrise (Book 3) by Kay Correll

Sweet Illusions (Book 4) by Jeanette Lewis

Sweet Regrets (Book 5) by Jennifer Peel

Sweet Rendezvous (Book 6) by Danielle Stewart

Sweet Saturdays (Book 7) by Pamela Kelley

Sweet Beginnings (Book 8) by Melissa McClone

Sweet Starlight (Book 9) by Kay Correll

Sweet Forgiveness (Book 10) by Jean Oram (Zoe's story!)

Sweet Reunion (Book 11) by Stacy Claflin

Sweet Entanglement (Book 12) by Jean C. Gordon

ABOUT THE AUTHOR

Jean Oram is a *New York Times* and *USA Today* bestselling romance author. Inspiration for her small town series came from her own upbringing on the Canadian prairies. Although, so far, none of her characters have grown up in an old schoolhouse or worked on a bee farm. Jean still lives on the prairie with her husband, two kids, and big shaggy dog where she can be found out playing in the snow or hiking.

Do you have questions, feedback, or just want to say hi? Connect with me:

Become an Official Fan: www.facebook.com/ groups/jeanoramfans
Newsletter: www.jeanoram.com/FREEBOOK
Facebook: www.facebook.com/JeanOramAuthor
Instagram: www.instagram.com/author_JeanOram

Website & blog: www.jeanoram.com

Thanks for reading.
XO
Jean